YOU GOT TO PAY TO PLAY

YOU GOT TO PAY TO PLAY

MEISHA CAMM

www.urbanbooks.net

Urban Books
1199 Straight Path
West Babylon, NY 11704

ISBN-13: 978-1-60162-085-9
ISBN-10: 1-60162-085-3

First Printing February 2009
Printed in the United States of America

10 9 8 7 6 5 4 3 2 1

Distributed by Kensington Publishing Corp.
Submit Wholesale Orders to:
Kensington Publishing Corp.
C/O Penguin Group (USA) Inc.
Attention: Order Processing
405 Murray Hill Parkway
East Rutherford, NJ 07073-2316
Phone: 1-800-526-0275
Fax: 1-800-227-9604

Acknowledgments

I want to thank Jesus Christ for giving me this gift of writing. With the power of prayer and determination, anything is possible.

The easiest part of a book is actually writing it. I have learned struggle, hard work and patience are three vital elements in the process of becoming successful.

Thank you to Carl Weber, Natalie Weber, my editor Nicole Peters and the entire Urban Books family for believing in my work, once again.

Most importantly, special thanks go out to all of the fans. Thank you for the feedback and encouragement.

Thank you to my parents Rodney and Shelly Camm, my daughter Shamaya, and my sister, Melanie for the encouragement and support. To Jessica Tilles and Niko Hamm, thank you for pushing and pushing me to write to the best of my ability and critiquing my work.

To my friends and family: Mr. and Mrs. Ballinger, Tiffany Ballinger, Carla Harrison, Malita Manning, Daneisha Elsbery, Keisha Bailey, Vickie Kennedy, Janie Harrison, Lance Cody, Raena and Stephen Simmons, Kisha Dodson, Tracy Davis, Adam Cottrell, Chrissy Smith, Sara Schiable, Linda Potts, Pat Howell, Kisha Powell, Vera Redd, the entire Wade family, Darrick Person and Renee Bobbs, thank you for your kind words of encouragement.

To the online writing groups RealSistaWriters and writersrx, thank you for always sending me important information pertaining to the book world. A special thanks to Gevell Wagner for taking the time out to read my work.

To Nikki Turner, Tobias Fox, Eddwin and Ernest McNair, Michael Baisden, Shannon Holmes, Zane, and Mary Monroe, thank you for steering me in the right direction.

This book is dedicated to my friend, Sprite.
You made it out alive.

Prologue

Sometimes I wish I could speed through time. To fly past seconds, minutes, hours—even days—would simply make my day. When I was little, I wished to set time so Mom could stay at home with me all day and not have to go to work. When I was in high school, I used to wish I could set my watch to miss each everlasting European history class. Right now, I want to surpass this moment. I'm in a five-star hotel on a king-size bed with a man I hardly know penetrating me with his pencil-size dick. My vagina can't take all this poking around. How did I come to this? More importantly, how can I change?

Chapter 1

"All right, Isabel Preston, let me see it," Mom requested as soon as I jumped off the last step of the bus.

"Let you see what?" I asked, clinching the straps of my Rainbow Brite book bag.

"Girl, you better stop playing with me. Now, hand over that report card. I don't brag 'bout you for nothing," she requested, zipping down my book bag.

"Mom, may I just say one thing before you look it?"

"Go ahead, but make it quick."

"I hope Daddy and you bought a better gift than last quarter."

"We'll see about that, Izzy."

"But, Mom," I whined.

"Hush, now while I'm looking at your grades," she insisted rummaging through my bag.

"Where's Daddy?" I asked over and over again, knowing it would annoy her. He and I were close as can be. Swimming, skating, fishing, teaching me how to ride bikes, going to the park or just playing in our backyard are just some of the things that we did together. I'm truly a daddy's girl and definitely listened to him more than my mother.

"Izzy, I'm so proud of you. Three As and two Bs; I will accept that any day," Mom exclaimed. The game in my house when it came to getting good grades was simple: Bringing home As earned you ten dollars for each. Bs were five dollars each.

"My savings account will be accepting forty dollars for a deposit."

"Let me do the math, young lady," she insisted while figuring the amount owed to me in her head. Mathematics was not one of my mother's better subjects.

"Where's Daddy?" I asked for the fifth time.

"He's on his way from work, only making one pit stop at the fish store. I'm making your favorite, broiled whiting, rice and peas, and candied yams."

"Thank you," I said, smiling, giving her a hug.

"You deserve it, baby," she said as we started walking into the house.

"So when am I going to get my money?" I asked, looking at her wallet.

"As soon as I can get to my wallet," she giggled.

"Thanks, Mom. I can't wait for Daddy to get home."

Daddy is going to be so proud of me. He is constantly reminding me about the value of a good education. Daddy is from Montego Bay, Jamaica. My father is the youngest of three children. Along with a sister and older brother, he didn't have a lot growing up. He made a promise to himself to get a good education so that he could do something positive with his life and he kept that promise. Daddy made it out of Jamaica and doesn't like to visit much. He says it's too many bad memories. Daddy never knew his father well and his mother died of cancer when they were teenagers. We've been to visit twice that

I can remember. His sister, Aunt Paula, had more babies than she can count and his brother, Uncle Ellis, was in a prison serving life for murder. We've never been back since.

Daddy and I are more alike, being strong-headed and having hot tempers. Plus, I had a mouth on me. Maybe I was more hardheaded too, because Mom was always beating my behind for talking back. She always says that I was the leader of my pack of friends. I will admit I could make them do just about anything in the name of fun. Mom also stressed about the consequences of my mouth and my actions. "Isabel Preston, child, you just can't say anything out your mouth and do whatever you feel like," she complained time and time again.

Mom only calls me Isabel Preston if she's got something to say. Believe me, she always has something to say. She is from the Popular Hall area of Norfolk. She is biracial, as she would have me call it. If you ask me, she's mixed and came out with kinky, curly hair and I have the same texture. To provide relief to Mom's fingers with all the combing and straightening of our hair, she rotates the days I get mine done. Her father, Edward, I've never seen because he doesn't come around much. I ask questions about him and where can I find him, but my questions go ignored or changed to another subject. Grandmother Elaine made excuses for him but Mom told me the truth. It is one of the things I always loved about her. Back then, mixed couples were not accepted into society. His family looked down upon Grandma Elaine and her family because of her skin color. Still, he chose to marry her. To this day, neither one has filed for divorce. Seventeen years has passed since both Mom and Grandma Elaine have seen him. It hurts to know your own grandfather doesn't want anything to do with you, your mother, and grandmother.

After both of my parents graduated from Norfolk State University, they got married in a small chapel and then came me. Mom is an X-ray technician for Sentara Leigh Hospital and Daddy is a longshoreman. A little sister or brother would be nice but my parents tell me they can't afford to have any more children. They scrimped and saved all their money so we can afford to live in a house in the middle-class Bellmont area, a community right off of Military Highway.

I'm in the seventh grade and three months away from the summer. My parents are sending me away to camp. I'm counting the days. Alicia, Rachel, and Vera are all coming with me. There's a huge campsite in the city of Suffolk. It's only about thirty minutes so I won't be too homesick. This is the third year that all of us have been spending our summers at camp.

Growing up, we had the same babysitter and never lost contact. Vera, who is my best friend, and I both live in Bellmont, while Alicia and Rachel live in Green Lakes Manor. Now, we all go to the same school. Vera's parents are still together just like mine. I am closer to her than the rest of the girls. Wherever I go, she goes and vice versa. Last year, Vera beat up Roxanne Bison for me because she threw a filled milk carton at my head. Middle school isn't easy. I don't get it. Girls hate me because they don't know me. Sometimes, I think these green eyes are a curse. After Vera gave her a few licks, I kicked her in the stomach a few times. Since I started school, Mom always taught me if anybody hits me, hit them back and tell the teacher to call her. Since Mom was college friends with the assistant principal and we didn't actually start the fight, Vera and I got off with warnings.

Alicia's and Rachel's parents were well-to-do. They both always had the latest clothes, shoes, hair accessories, and had their noses stuck up just a little. Her parents had an established bookkeeping business. Alicia, especially, couldn't help calling me to brag about all the new things she got. If Vera and I got anything new, which was rare, she was jealous. We never could understand that. She had more things than we ever did. Alicia was spoiled and if she didn't get her way, the world was coming to an end. Once, while all of us were over her house watching a movie, eating popcorn and drinking Fanta grape soda, she slapped her mother in the face for picking up the wrong movie. Her father always looked the other way because he was too busy trying to please his precious daughter. My behind would have been close to dead getting whoopings from both of my parents and my Grandmother Elaine. Rachel's father was the vice president of a computer company. He taught us all a lot about computers. She was concerned about getting more as than anyone at the school and being first for everything.

Chapter 2

It was getting late and *Entertainment Tonight* was coming on. I had to be in bed by nine o'clock. My homework was done. Daddy should have been home by now, I thought. Mom had become impatient waiting around for him to cook and for us to eat as a family. She ended up cooking salmon with the rice and candied yams. I didn't mind. I had my forty dollars, which help me work up an appetite. Plus, she let me eat my dinner while watching *The Fresh Prince of Bel-Air* in the living room. She didn't eat much. Her eyes were glued to the window and the telephone. After dinner, I ate one scoop of strawberry ice cream and a slice of red velvet cake.

Chapter 3

"Izzy, why don't you go take your shower?" she instructed, pacing the floor with her arms folded.

"No, I'm waiting for Daddy," I replied while watching the television.

"Girl, what did I say?" Mom ordered, inching closer to me.

"At this time, Daddy wouldn't make me take a shower. Besides, NBC is showing an extra episode of *The Fresh Prince of Bel-Air* and I'm watching it," I demanded while folding my arms.

"You're not watching the show," she replied while smacking her right hand in my mouth.

"All right," I surrendered with tears coming down my eyes.

"Dry up those tears right now before I smack you in the mouth again. If you want to talk back to me in my house, your behind will pay for the consequences. Child, when will you ever learn? Izzy, I pray to God every night for you not to find yourself in a bad situation because of the choices that you make," she preached.

As I walked down the hall and into the bathroom to start the water, I began to worry. Where is my Daddy? Is he okay? Could he have gotten hurt at work? Vera's father works with Daddy and got hurt on the job. He was out of work for six months. If he did ever get hurt, maybe I can get a job to help out.

After turning the water off, I heard Mom coming down the hallway and started calling my name.

"Isabel, come into the living room when you get out of the bathroom."

"All right," I yelled back.

"What did I tell you about yelling in my house?" she scolded.

"Sorry," I replied. It didn't take me long to dry off and get in my pink pajamas. I ran down the hall.

"Yes, Mom." I approached, entering the living room.

"Sit down, baby, there's something I want to tell you." She let out a big sigh while I sat down. "While you were in the shower, your Uncle Ronnie just called. Your father is living with him, for now."

"Why?" I pleaded. "Well, things haven't been the best between your father and me. We may need some time apart to figure things out. Daddy is still going to come pick you up on the weekends."

"Why didn't he come tell me himself?"

"Honey, I don't know. All I do know is that I'm here, your aunts and uncles and your grandmother are here for you. We will get through anything. Most of all, we have God," she explained, pointing to the King James Bible lying on the kitchen counter.

"I still don't understand why Daddy would just pick up and leave us like this." Tears began to run down my face. "I hate him!" I screamed, running into my room to get refuge from all this confusion and unanswered questions, and landing on my bed. Mom was in fast pursuit.

"Now, you listen to me young lady. Your father loves you and me. We are just having a hard time right now. Izzy, you're too young to understand love, marriage, and all of its complications. When you get older—"

"Why are you defending him? Daddy didn't even have the decency to call you or me. It's been on the calendar for months that I would be getting my report card. He doesn't care about me," I screamed, cutting her off.

"Get some rest, please. You're upset, I'm upset. Plus, you have to go to school tomorrow morning," she explained, looking at her watch. She kneeled down to the bed to give me a hug. I pushed her away.

"Good night," she cooed, turning off my lamp. I grabbed Neal, my brown baby teddy bear who's been my side since the day I was born. I cried until I fell asleep.

Chapter 4

"Are you sure that you want to miss the slumber party of the year?" Rachel asked while filing her nails.

"Yes, I wish I could come but my father is picking me up," I replied anxiously, waiting for the school bell to ring. We only had fifteen minutes left. I was grateful for the weekend, especially this one. It was Memorial Day weekend, which meant we were out for a three-day weekend and I get to spend more time with my father. The bell rang.

"Do you want me to wait for you?" Rachel asked, eagerly wanting to get out of the classroom.

"No, go ahead because I don't want you to miss the bus. Plus, Daddy should be waiting outside for me in his car," I explained, putting papers into my book bag.

"Call me later." She smiled and waved good-bye, heading toward the door.

"All right," I replied. I was so excited about spending some time with Daddy, wondering what we were going to do first. Maybe we could go bowling. Two years ago, I remember throwing a strike three times in a row. Or maybe we could head to my Uncle Ronnie's house, who always kept me laughing with his jokes.

As I stepped outside, the buses filled with kids were heading out. After the dust settled, I looked around for Daddy's Ford 150 dark green truck. *Maybe he's running late,* I thought, looking down at my watch.

Chapter 5

Two hours later, feeling ashamed and abandoned, I sat on the curb with my head down with countless tears running down my face. I could hear a car coming toward me. It was Mom's gray Toyota Corolla. After an hour and forty-five minutes of waiting, the janitor let me use the phone to call Mom at work to come pick me up. The way I felt, I could have walked home, but Mom wasn't going to allow it. Now, I regret even picking up the phone.

"Hey," she whispered, handing me a Kleenex, trying not to upset me even more.

"Hi," I answered, putting my seat belt on.

"Do you want to go to Rachel's party after all?" she asked with a slight smile on her face, not wanting to face the next inevitable question while making a right turn out of the parking lot.

"No, I'm not up for any company right now. Did he call?"

"No, I called his job. He wasn't there. Then I called

your Uncle Ronnie's house and just kept getting the answering machine. I'm sure he has a good reason for all of this."

"That's what you said the last time and the time before and the time before that. I haven't seen Daddy since the day you told me he moved out. Why does he keep promising to get me but never shows up?" I asked, crying.

"I don't know, honey," she replied, crying.

"You continue to make excuses for him over and over again. Why? To tell the truth, does he not love us anymore? Does he have another family and forgot about us?" I asked.

"No, honey, he is confused about some things right now. Don't worry, this will pass and we will go back to being a family. I'm off for the rest of the day. We can do some fun things together. How about a bag of blueberry cotton candy? That always cheers you up," she suggested.

"Mom, take me home. I want to be by myself," I stated, looking out the passenger side window.

Later that night, Daddy called to speak with me. Mom begged me to at least come to the phone and hear him out, but I couldn't. I didn't even want to talk to him. All I would get is a whole bunch of excuses.

The next day, Grandma Elaine came to stay with us. She was keeping me company while Mom went to work. It was a bright, sunny Saturday morning. Looking out the window, I noticed the birds were chirping, a mother duck and her six ducklings were crossing the street, and the bunnies were hopping across the yard. I woke up to the smell of Folgers roasted-blend coffee (Grandma's favorite). After I brushed my teeth and used the bathroom, I ran downstairs to the kitchen to greet Grandma. She was hard at work preparing pancakes, turkey bacon, and eggs.

"How's my little girl doing?" she asked as I hugged her.

"I'm so glad you're here," I said, sneaking a piece of bacon off the plate.

"Last night, you didn't want to talk to your father. He's going to call again tonight," Mom said, entering the kitchen.

"Mom, he sounds funny on the phone."

"How so?" she asked.

"Well, he talks really fast and he says the same thing over and over again."

"He's trying to make things right between us all."

"Daddy is trying to make things right. How can you say that, Mom?" I asked, mocking her.

"Watch it, Isabel Preston," Mom said.

"You hardly spend any time with me or Grandma anymore because you're always working. When Daddy does get around to calling us, you act as if he's the king of the world or something. You're so weak. Why can't you stand up to him? I don't need a when-I-feel-like-it father and that seems all right to you the way he treats us."

"Izzy, that's enough. Your mouth and your actions are always getting you in trouble. You surely don't see now, but when you get older, your choices will get you into a situation you can't so easily get out of." Grandma stated giving me a stern look. By the way her eyes looked I knew if I said another word, I was going to get knocked across the floor and end up in the living room.

"I'm off to work to pick up some more overtime hours," Mom whimpered, leaving the kitchen and walking toward the front door. Deep down, I didn't feel bad for what I said. I had to get it off my chest. Later on that day, Alicia, Rachel, and Vera came over. We went to Military Circle Mall to get a slice of pizza and pick up a few bottles of nail polish from Woolworth.

Chapter 6

Mom picked up another job working at the grocery store as a night manager. Daddy must not be helping out with the bills. He wasn't staying with Uncle Ronnie any more either. The last we heard from him was four months ago. When Mom was not working, she was usually pacing the floor and praying to Jesus. Something deep was bothering her. I had a gut feeling she knew where Daddy was all this time. I would ask her over and over again where he was. She would simply reply, "baby, I don't know." It is hurtful as a child to know your mother can lie in your face not once but plenty of times about the whereabouts of your father.

Over the next several months, I was spending more time at my grandmother's house. Maybe it hurt her to know how bad I was feeling about Daddy leaving us. This particular Sunday afternoon was rainy and humid. Grandma didn't believe in the air conditioner. She would always say, "Izzy, you won't ever miss what you never had." As I went into each room to try to cool off, I was faced with fans of hot air blowing on my sticky skin. Finally, I gave up and headed to the kitchen to grab a tall glass of ice. That should cool me down, I thought, wiping the sweat from my forehead with a cloth.

"You missed a good service this morning," Grandma Elaine said as I stepped into the kitchen. Shirley Caesar's song, "Time To Be Blessed," was playing on the radio. She played gospel music all day, every day, especially on Sundays.

"What was Pastor Sears preaching about?" I inquired, reaching for the ice in the freezer.

"Well, he was talking about hope and forgiveness," she replied while handing me a plastic cup.

"Yeah, two things I can't do right now, Grandma," I explained, pouring the ice into the cup.

"Baby, listen to me. I know things are hard between you and your mother and you and your father. I'm here for you whenever you need me. You're just a little girl caught in the middle of your daddy's foolishness. Despite everything going on, can you do one thing for me?"

"Sure, Grandma, I would do anything for you," I broadcasted, plopping down into the kitchen chair.

"Don't give up on your parents. Your mother is just trying to make sense of this, herself. She feels guilty about everything and you don't make it any easier on her, Isabel. Lately, I've been noticing your tone of voice with your mother. I don't like it. You will give her the respect that she deserves."

"Mom acts like all she cares about is Daddy and when is he coming home. Well, maybe he's never coming home," I blurted out.

"Izzy, you heard what I said."

"Yes, Grandma," I replied, putting my head down. The next song that played on the radio was Shirley Caesar again with her song, "Revive Us Again."

"After you finish with that cup of ice, come help me with this crabmeat. I've already put the breading and spices into it. Now, all I want you to do is put it in individual patties."

"Yes, ma'am. Grandma, today is Sunday. I thought we were having our usual. Don't get me wrong, I love your roast chicken, sweet potatoes with marshmallows, and string beans. Plus, I can't wait to get a tall glass of your raspberry lemonade."

"Thanks, baby. Today, I got a taste for baked crab cakes with my homemade cocktail sauce. After we finish cooking and eating, later on, I want you and I to try our best to eat that watermelon sitting on the kitchen floor."

That same night, I woke up to use the bathroom. I overheard Grandma and Mom talking, Mom was crying and made the painful confession to Grandma that she was the same age as me when her father left. Grandma and Mom couldn't help but wonder if history was repeating itself.

Chapter 7

As long as my grades continued to stay on the honor roll, Mom allowed me to work as a bagger at the grocery store. I'm trying to save up for a car. In a few months, I will be turning sixteen. *Nothing too expensive, just something to get me from point A to point B,* I thought. My goal is to save five thousand dollars. I hope that will be enough to buy a car. I didn't want to have a monthly payment.

It's been five years and counting since Daddy walked out on us. Although Mom wanted to buy me my first car, these days all she could ever worry about were bills; when they're coming in and when or how they are going to get paid. Mom always seemed to find a way to pay everything and worked hard to maintain our lifestyle. There was never a time when our house would be taken away. Sure, I didn't get the latest designer fashions but at least I had a roof over my head, the lights were on, and food was on the table. When push came to shove, she took care of me by herself. Could I have the strength to one day do the same if I had to?

After working at the store for three months, I had to admit my mother was a great supervisor. My mother wasn't my direct supervisor but I watched her interact with her direct employees. She was caring and had an open-door policy to whoever needed to talk about anything. Plus, she didn't breathe down their throats every second even if they did something wrong. Not to mention, Mom ran weekly contests to the employee who gave the best customer service; they would win the prize of getting off an hour earlier. Other coworkers didn't hesitate coming up to me explaining how they felt I was so lucky to have a mother like her. I had a new respect for my Mom but I could never admit it to her. Despite it all, I took it all in stride. Somehow, I couldn't see myself working the next thirty years like my mother was doing and my grandmother did. Grandmother Elaine cleaned homes for a living. But I didn't want to be a stay-at-home mom and housewife. To be honest, I didn't know what I wanted to be when I grow up.

Although I was still trying to figure out what to do with the rest of my life, Mom already had a definitive idea. Every chance she gets, Mom is nagging me about going to college. She has asked me numerous times to round up applications but I didn't. After several weeks of begging, Mom took matters in her own hands to get the applications herself. When I got home, paperwork from various schools such as North Carolina A&T, Virginia Wesleyan, Norfolk State, Hampton, as well as Bennett and Spelman Colleges, were all splattered on the kitchen floor. I was in no mood for college talk tonight. Today was Friday and I had only one thing on my mind: partying.

* * *

"Hey, Mom," I said, entering the kitchen and heading toward the Cookie Monster cookie jar for two Oreos.

"Hi, baby. You have no more excuses. Here are some college applications. Start filling them out today. It's important that you get your applications in early," she explained, stirring sugar in her coffee and flipping through *Jet* magazine.

"Mom, I'm not going to college," I stated frankly. Mom had her heart set on me going to college. I had my heart set on her standing up to Daddy. It's been five years since he's been gone and I haven't seen her do it yet. She still refused to date another man because she still believed Daddy was going to come back and save the day. Mom desperately needs to face reality and get out of that fantasy world of hers. I think there is a good man out there for Mom. He could be cutting the grass, taking the trash out, and paying for at least half of these bills for the house. Then maybe she won't have to work two jobs anymore.

"Isabel, you're going to college. Girl, you graduate next year. You should've started filling out applications months ago. Before you leave this house and take my car out for a joyride with your friends, you better have at least two applications filled out. When you finish, give them to me so I can review. Don't worry about taking them to the post office. I want to make sure they get back to the colleges and not end up in your drawer."

"I only have an hour and a half to get dressed and pick up all the girls."

"Well, you better start writing. Procrastination isn't one of your better characteristics," she stated, dangling the car keys in her hands.

"Fine," I replied, picking up two applications and heading out of the kitchen and marching upstairs, running to my room, and slamming the door as hard as I could.

"Isabel Preston, we don't slam doors in this house," Mom announced for the hundredth time.

Pissed off and pressed for time, I managed to get the college applications to Virginia Wesleyan and Hampton University completed. Forty-five minutes was all it took for me to get ready. I've had my peach satin dress hanging in the closet patiently waiting for me to get into it. Vera, Rachel, Alicia, and I were all wearing satin dresses that gently hung off our shoulders. Vera was wearing the color red. Rachel loved the color sky blue and Alicia would be showing off a green dress. Rushing down the stairs, I began to wonder if I my hair would stay in place and if my makeup was done to perfection. A caramel skin tone, green eyes, curly hair, and a Coca-Cola bottle–shaped body would have those guys' heads rolling. I didn't even bother to say bye to Mom as she handed me the car keys.

"Tonight is a rare exception. Normally, your behind would be in this house by ten o'clock on the dot. I went ahead and made the call. *The Spirit of Norfolk* should be docking at midnight. I'm graciously giving you forty minutes to drop those girls off and be in this house. Don't make me come looking for you. Just in case you are late, I have my prayer team ready to go. Ms. Harrison across the street said it would be no problem if I wanted to use her van," she explained while rummaging through her purse.

"Anything else?" I asked while rolling my eyes and crossing my arms, still wondering why she didn't stay on Daddy like she did me.

"Besides changing that nasty attitude you have, there is one thing."

"Yes?" I questioned with built-up agitation in my voice.

"Smile, girl, you look just like your momma tonight," she instructed while holding a Kodak camera.

After picking up all the girls, I managed to get on Interstate 64 heading toward downtown Norfolk. As we grooved to Salt-N-Pepa's song, "Push It," I turned up the radio volume. Next came the song, "Computer Love" by Zapp and "Lean on Me" by Club Nouveau followed. *The Sprit of Norfolk* was docked in the Elizabeth River. It stood more than sixty feet high. We arrived twenty minutes early. I dreaded us getting left behind. Not surprising, some other students were already there, waiting to get on the boat. It was a rather warm March night.

The captain let the late stragglers have another fifteen minutes to get on the boat. This school dance would be the most talked about for the whole entire year. The boat was huge inside. An elegant ballroom and dining area stretched as long as half of our football field. The food was served buffet style with baked chicken and fish, steamed vegetables, and dinner rolls with sweet cream butter. As for finger foods, there were plenty of vegetable and fruit trays including watermelons, kiwi, and mangoes, all served on silver plates. Also, cheese with crackers, ham biscuits, drumsticks, and tangy sweet Swedish meatballs were served as appetizers. For beverages, there was a choice of water, sparkling Welch's grape juice, and tea.

The girls and I were all huddled in the corner when Principal Samson made an announcement at the mic.

"Okay, welcome to our first annual dance on the *Sprit of Norfolk*. Let's give a round of applause for the employees of the ship. The food was fantastic," he said while rubbing his stomach. The crowd cheered on. "We're going to have a good time tonight. As you know, I have a few rules I want each and everyone of you to keep in mine. Keep your hands to yourself, keep it fun, and keep your attitude in check." DJ Rock started playing music.

The guys were checking us out while we were checking them out. I didn't have anyone in mind that I wanted to talk to. Most of the guys at my school were immature and silly. While my back was turned toward the crowd, someone tapped me on the shoulder. Turning around, I realized it was none other than my summer camp sweetheart, Russell Carton. The guy was a little on the scrawny side but his humor made up for it. He was 50 percent of the reason why I continued to return to the camp.

"Russell, what are you doing here?" I asked while hugging him.

"Izzy, you still have those green eyes. I could get lost in them. I couldn't miss the March dance. My grandmother is very sick so Dad thought it would be best if we move back to Norfolk so we could be close to her. I start at Lake Taylor High School first thing Monday morning as a senior," he expressed, getting back to the subject at hand.

"I'm glad to hear you'll be at my school. We may be in some classes together."

"Do you mind if we go upstairs to the second floor? It's so loud in here."

"Sure," I replied. The girls all winked at me while Russell lead the way to the second floor.

* * *

It was quiet and calm upstairs while Russell and I overlooked the water. At first, both of us were too shy to speak so we continued to look at each other and just smile.

"After all these years, I still wonder how you're doing."

"Me too. So will you have enough credits to graduate from Lake Taylor?"

"As far as I know, we're here to stay. It's the neighborhood where my father grew up on. Plus, my mother loves the area we live in. Not to mention, I will be graduating with you."

"What's your plans for college?"

"I applied at North Carolina A & T and Rutgers University. How about you?" he asked, nudging closer to me.

"I'm not sure if I want to go to college. My mother is forcing me to fill out applications. In fact, one of the stipulations for me to come tonight was to have at least two applications done. I randomly picked Hampton University and Virginia Wesleyan."

"What does your father think about your decision?"

"Daddy doesn't know or care. He isn't around anymore."

"I can hear the hurt in your voice. I'm here for you, Izzy."

"You are?" I asked while my head found refuge on his chest. I began to briefly explain to him what happened to my family. It felt good to have a listening ear.

Next, Russell gently caressed my chin. He motioned my lips to meet his. We kissed for what seemed at least for an hour. To my disgust and irritation, one of Principal Samson's chaperones spotted us lip-locking.

"What was Principal Samson's first rule?" he asked while approaching us with a bright flashlight.

"Keep our hands to ourselves," Russell and I said in unison.

"This is a warning. I don't want to see you two kids tongue-tied again."

Between Friday and Tuesday morning, I talked to Russell on the phone every chance I got. On Monday, I got a nasty stomach virus that lasted for a day. Mom said it might have been in the air. She nagged me even more to get the college applications filled out. I couldn't wait to go to school just to get the ten minutes to spend with him between classes. Arriving at school, people began staring at me. *Do I have something on my face or in my nose? Did I remember to put deodorant on?* I thought. By third bell, the guys were whistling at me and the girls were shaking their heads. I was going to find out what was going on. One of my guy buddies would tell me the truth.

"Brian, do you know why the whole school is staring at me as if I killed someone and got away with it?" I asked while he plopped himself in the desk.

"Izzy, I've been trying to call you all weekend."

"Mom gave me your messages, but I was spending most of my time on the phone with Russell."

"That's the problem."

"What do you mean? Russell just got to the school."

"Well, he's trying to make a name for himself. He told Ervin, the guy with the biggest mouth in school, that he had sex with you on the second floor of the *Spirit of Norfolk,* Friday night."

"What? Are you sure?" I asked while my stomach began to ache.

"Izzy, we've been friends since we were two years old. I wouldn't tell you something like that if I wasn't certain. He even told me and twenty other guys in the locker room this morning that he slept with you. Do you know how many guys wish you would just breathe on them for a second? You're the girl with the green eyes. When I heard it, I punched Russell three times in the face. Luckily, the other guys broke it up before the coach came in. Now my girlfriend, Tiffany is pissed at me because she thinks I like you," he explained, shaking his head.

"Because you fought for me," I finished, cutting him off.

"You're like a little sister to me. Plus, I can't stand when a guy brags about having sex with a woman."

"Brian, thank you for defending me. I'll smooth things over with Tiffany. The girl is not a hothead so I hope she will see reason. I wish you would have punched Russell fifty more times in the face." Twenty minutes into history class, I excused myself to the bathroom.

"You got fifteen minutes to use the bathroom," Ms. Horrister shot back at me as I headed toward the door with my purse.

With my palms sweaty, I headed to the cafeteria. *Everyone knew—the cafeteria workers and the janitors take their smoke break right about now,* I thought, looking down at my watch. Dashing into the cafeteria without being seen, I picked up the sharpest knife I could find in the kitchen. Janitors assign all the lockers to the students so I headed to their office and got the combination for Russell's locker. Looking down at my watch, I had only eight more minutes to be back in class. I stayed calm while briskly walking through the school halls.

"How's it going, Isabel?" Principal Samson asked while stopping me in my tracks.

"Things are great. I'm just headed back to my history class."

"Have a great day. By the way, you're on the honor roll. Congratulations—straight As again."

"Thank you, Principal Samson," I responded.

After he was out of sight, I kept my eye on the prize. Russell's locker was coming up. The locker door opened with ease and I placed the knife in. One last stop to the pay phone outside, I put my jacket over the phone receiver and requested to speak with the Principal Samson. I disguised my voice and gave him an anonymous tip about what was in Russell's locker. Luckily, I made it back to history class on the dot.

Russell was expelled from all of the Norfolk's schools. I knew the surrounding cities Portsmouth, Suffolk, Virginia Beach, and Chesapeake wouldn't take him in their school districts. People thought it was for retaliation for Brian kicking his behind. The news spread quickly throughout the school. Once Brian's older brothers found out, they too beat Russell's ass. This sensational story took the heat off of me. Two days later, Russell called me to try to explain his side of the story. I wasn't interested and screamed at him for spreading lies that I spread my legs on the ship. Russell was advised to never call my house again. Besides, he had bigger problems. For instance, the city of Norfolk charged him with having a deadly weapon on school property. Plus, his school record was on the line and last, but not least, jail time could be a real possibility.

Chapter 8

Two weeks ago, I graduated from Lake Taylor as class valedictorian. Everyone was at the ceremony except for Daddy. Deep down, I was hoping he would have the decency to show up, but I knew that was only asking too much of my father nowadays.

Now that I'm out of school I should be having fun with my friends before they all leave for college. Instead, I am helping to take care of my mother who has come down with a terrible cold. The city of Norfolk was going through a tremendous heat wave. Luckily, we had an air conditioner at our house, but because of it, the cold air blowing in my mother's direction at night only gave her a headache and a fever the next morning. I took her car and ran to the drugstore to grab her medicine.

"Nice legs," a voice said as I got out of my mother's vehicle.

"Nice car," I responded, looking at his black Mercedes-Benz as he was approaching me.

"How did you know it was my car?" he asked.

"I saw the lights flash while you pressed the alarm button."

"You're a good observer and pretty too. Your eyes are making me lose my train of thought."

How many times have I heard that? I thought.

"Thanks for the compliment. Have a good night, sir."

"Sir? Do I look old to you, green eyes?"

"Is your car black?" I asked.

"Do you want to take it for a ride?"

"No," I lied.

"My name is Bruce Tripson. I'm twenty-seven years old and would love to take you out," he introduced, trying to reach for my hand to shake it. Bruce was the type that I dreamed of. LL Cool J lips, Action Jackson's body, nice pearly-white teeth and light brown eyes. I'm a sucker for light brown eyes. He even had a tattoo on his right arm that read *RIP Timothy*.

"My name is Isabel, not green eyes. I'm barely eighteen. You just beat possible statutory rape charges by three months. I would prefer not to shake your hand. I don't know where that hand has been," I added.

"Girl, has anyone ever said to you that you got a smart mouth?"

"Have you ever told another woman that she was pretty?"

"To be so young, you're very hostile. Go out with me one time. If you're not enjoying yourself within thirty minutes, I'll take you right back home," he said with a smirk on his face.

"Well, all right, but make it twenty minutes," I surrendered, giving in to his proposition. I got back into the car to look for a piece of paper and a pen. *I haven't had any male company in a while,* I thought.

"When do you want to go out? And try hard not to answer me with a question."

"Saturday night," I responded.

"It's two days away and I don't think I can wait that long."

"Hey, Saturday or never."

"All right, I'll do my best to occupy my time."

Chapter 9

"Mom, you can talk to me till I'm blue in the face, I'm not going to college. Plus, you can't make me," I called out. Grandma Elaine was here as the referee. I knew my mother wanted to choke me. I loved the fact I was getting underneath her skin. Seeing Mom cringing at me was more priceless than five college degrees.

"Is it that grown-ass man you've been seeing? Has he filled your head with this nonsense about you not going to college?" she inquired. Bruce had been calling the house at least five or six times a day. I told Mom to let me have my own line; that way, she wouldn't have to hear the phone ring. She refused. Not to mention, for the past month Bruce has been sending flowers, teddy bears, and chocolates to the house.

"No," I replied in my most pleasant voice.

"Izzy, is any of this getting through to you?" she inquired, looking into my eyes.

I admit I was going to miss the girls. Vera, who served as a cheerleader all throughout high school, was going to

Rutgers University on a full athletic scholarship. Rachel was attending Norfolk State University. At sixteen, Alicia was diagnosed with a thyroid condition that made her gain about fifty pounds. Although she was on a strict diet and medical attention, that didn't stop her from getting a full scholarship at Hampton University.

"Yes, I'm listening to you." I literally meant just *listening* because I wasn't going to do anything about her forceful attempts to make me go to college. "Besides, you graduated from college and still have to work two jobs to make ends meat."

"I do what I need to do for this family."

"Do you like my earrings?" I asked, trying to change the subject.

"Yes, but what I don't like is each time you walk outta here to see that man, your shorts and skirts get shorter and shorter. My gut is telling me that he isn't good for you. This is what I'm talking about, Isabel Preston. The choice you're making to be with this man isn't a good one. You don't even know him or what he's capable of. He's too old and he's just wants to screw you, baby. You're worth more than that."

"Whatever. Mom, you're just mad because Daddy doesn't want you anymore. Hmm, let me see, it's going on year six, right?" I shot back at her. Before I knew it, Mom slapped me across the face. Before I knew what I was doing, I slapped her back.

"Izzy, if you hit your mom one more time, I will beat your tail so bad. We didn't raise you to act like this," Grandma yelled while getting between us before we could throw blows.

"Isabel, don't make me slap you again. No child of mine will sleep in my house and put her hands on me. Do it again and see what will happen to you. You will honor me or pay the consequences. I'm trying to save you from a lot of heartache and pain. Older men only want young girls so they can control them. But you don't want to listen to me, so go on out my damn door to be Bruce's whore for the night. The only time your ass wants to move is when that man calls. Girl, you don't even bother to call me to even let me know what you're doing or where you're at. I was hoping this was a phase you were going through but this *new* you isn't going away."

"Mom, leave Bruce out of this. It has nothing to do with him," I pleaded with a hint of fear in my voice. It's very rare for her to curse.

"Isabel, you got accepted to Virginia Wesleyan, Hampton University, and Bennett College on full scholarships. Do you know how many other young men and women would jump at the chance of a full scholarship? Girl, you got a free ride and you're throwing it all away."

"I don't want to go to school. Maybe I may change my mind next fall. In the meantime, I'm going to take it easy. Besides, getting *good* grades and being a *good* girl didn't bring my daddy back. You still won't tell me where or how to find him. You know where he is. All these years, you've been lying to my face about his whereabouts."

"I don't know where—" Mom pleaded.

"Mom, save it," I said cutting her off and heading toward the front door as I heard Bruce honk the horn. The tension in the room was thick. Out of the corner of my eye, I could see Grandma Elaine shaking her head.

"Girl, come in this house at a decent hour," she screamed in frustration.

As I walked to the car, I thought about our first date. It was at Doumar's, located on Monticello Avenue. It's an old-fashioned diner and has a drive-in. The wait to get served was only around ten minutes. Bruce and I didn't mind because the service is great. Plus, we were too busy enjoying our conversation. He ordered a BBQ sandwich, french fries, coleslaw, and a glass of cherry smash. A steak sandwich smothered in onions, French fries, and a strawberry milkshake was my choice for the night. After our drive-in dinner, we headed down to the oceanfront and rode bikes on the boardwalk. Luckily, Bruce bought me a pair of shorts, because he didn't want anyone looking up my skirt. The man is so good to me.

Chapter 10

Five months into this relationship, Bruce has been nothing but a gentleman. I've grown accustomed to the taste of having an older man. Eventually, he's going to want a taste of my pussy. Tonight, we're headed to the Aberdeen Barn, an upscale steak and seafood restaurant on Holiday Drive.

"What's wrong, baby?" I asked, as the waiter seated us at our booth.

"Today is my little brother's birthday, Timothy. He would have been twenty-one years old. Tonight, I should have been taking him to get drunk. I still have nightmares about not being able to get to the bedroom," Bruce explained with his hands clutched together.

Years ago, there was a fire in his family's apartment. Everyone was able to get out except Timothy. He was seven years old. The firemen held Bruce back as he made several attempts to get to his brother. Days later they found out that source of the fire was due to Bruce's mother smoking a cigarette in Timothy's room and lit ash fell on the highly flammable shag carpet. Bruce still has repeated nightmares about it. At times, I can hear him mumbling in his sleep. At the time of the accident, he was fifteen.

Before the fire, Bruce and his little brother worshipped the ground their mother walked on. She tried her best to instill her sons with the importance of treating a woman as a queen and being respectful. Unfortunately, Bruce had seen his father physically and mentally abuse his mother. I wonder what side will play out in our relationship. So far, so good.

"If Timothy was here, what would he order?" I asked, rubbing his shoulder, trying to cheer him up.

"Crab legs, that boy loved it."

"Hello, I'm Jorge, let me start off by telling you our specials," the waiter greeted.

"Jorge, that won't be necessary. We both know what we want."

"What will you two be having?"

"Two broiled seafood platters. The gentleman will have a shot of whiskey and I will have a Shirley Temple with three cherries. Both of us will have Caesar salads," I instructed.

"Very well," he replied while taking our menus.

"Izzy, you always know how to make me feel better."

"It's in honor for Timothy," I said, winking at him.

Later that night, back at Bruce's lavish apartment at Pembroke Square, both of us were in the mood to watch something funny. He had the latest entertainment center from Sony that had surround sound. His couch and love

seat were suede, so if he or I were wearing jeans, he preferred I'd take them off and put on sweatpants or shorts.
With such a small request, I didn't mind at all. We turned
the TV on just in time to watch *In Living Color*. After the
show, on the couch, Bruce pulled me close to him.

"Thank you for cheering me up."

"You're welcome," I said and kissed him. Just as our
tongues were about to touch, he stopped, got up from the
couch, and motioned for me to do the same.

"Izzy, it's been a while now that I've been seeing you
and things couldn't be better. Right now, all I want is to
feel inside of you. The sexual tension has been building
up and I don't want to fight it anymore," he said, caressing my chin.

"I don't want to fight it anymore, either," I responded,
slowly taking off all of my clothes. Slowly, I walked into
the bedroom as Bruce followed me with a trail of his
clothes behind him.

"Get a condom," I said.

"Not tonight. The next time, I'll slide one on. I just
want to feel you, please."

"If there's a next time," I giggled, lying down on the
bed. *He can't get me pregnant even if he wanted to. Three
months ago, I went to the free health clinic and was given a
long-lasting supply of birth control pills,* I thought. I knew
this day was coming so I wanted to be prepared.

"Girl, stop playing with me," he ordered.

"Please, don't ram it, this is my first time."

"Damn, I know your pussy is going to be tight. But
first, let me get you wet," he announced, reaching for a
bottle of baby oil.

Bruce pulled my legs down toward the edge of the
bed. He lifted them up, drizzled oil all over, and started
slowly rubbing in between my thighs. I relaxed my
shoulders and closed my eyes. He began to do it harder

and return back to the slow motion. Bruce started massaging my breasts. He climbed on top of me and started thrusting his pelvis into mine while sucking on my right breast. He nudged his fingers into my pussy, discovering how wet I was. Bruce rolled us into opposite positions.

"I'm going to make you to cum."

"Oh really?" I asked.

"You'll see. Get on top and follow my directions."

"All right," I replied to his commands.

"Lick the tip of my dick in circular motion. Try hard not to bite it. I'm quite sensitive down there."

"What's next?" I asked after ten minutes.

"Climb on top."

"Please, don't ram it in hard. I know it's going to hurt."

"Izzy, stop whining. You're going to kill the mood, baby." I slid down on his dick slowly. Bruce pulled my legs close to his chest. At first, it did hurt. Then, I began to feel a hot sensation and my pussy was dripping in wetness. I began rocking back and forth over and over again. Meanwhile, Bruce licked his second and third finger and started massaging my clitoris.

"Izzy, baby, you just don't know how good this feels."

"Tell me, how does it feel?" I asked, trying to keep up with the rocking. I was getting lost in the motion of his fingers. It felt so good what he was doing to me.

"It's something I can't put into words. Keep rocking, I'm going to cum," he whispered. Bruce grabbed my thighs and held on tight as he came. Unfortunately, I didn't come. *But there's always next time,* I thought.

Once I hopped into a hot shower, I began to think about a lot, particularly about Bruce and my family. Tonight, I knew before I left my mother's house, I wasn't coming back till the next day. Over and over again, Mom and I fight about the same subject: Bruce. She thinks he's no good for me. Grandma Elaine may feel the same but hasn't said as much as Mom. He makes me happy. Bruce and I made our relationship official last month. Shouldn't my happiness matter to Mom? All she wants me to do is sit in an empty house and hope for Daddy to come to his senses and walk in the door. Well, I gave up on that fantasy years ago. When is she going to do the same? I got smart and bought a whole suitcase full of clothes and a bagful of toiletries to leave over here. It's convenient and I'm marking my territory. I finished my shower and my thinking, pulled on a nightshirt, and slowly climbed into bed next to Bruce. He was already fast asleep. In a couple of seconds, so would I.

"Rise and shine, sleepyhead. Hurry up and get dressed. We have places to go and I'm hungry. Those silver-dollars pancakes, hash browns, and apple-smoked bacon from IHOP are calling me," Bruce said playfully, throwing a pillow at my head. I sleepily got out of the bed and proceeded to start the day. Once I finished all my morning duties I was ready to go within a half hour.

"Where to next?" I asked while we were leaving the IHOP parking lot. My belly was stuffed due to a hardy breakfast of buttermilk pancakes, eggs, and sausage.

"Izzy, we're going to look at some bikes. I know you love to ride them at the beach," Bruce replied playfully.

"Ha-ha, very funny," I replied, tapping his arm. Even though Bruce hasn't told me yet, it didn't take much to figure out what he does for a living. Only the drug life can you have the flexibility that he had. I loved the way

Bruce could come and go as he pleased. He was an entrepreneur and worked for himself. I admired it about him.

The next stop was Nissan Checkered Flag on Virginia Beach Boulevard. As we were approaching the office building, four car salesmen swarmed in to get our attention. Bruce denied each of their gestures to take a ride in anything on the lot. Instead, he requested the service of a guy named Rob. We continued to walk toward the building. Rob was finishing up with another client. We were asked to have a seat. After twenty minutes, Rob greeted us.

"Hello, I'm Rob. You must be Isabel. You're more beautiful in person than in a picture."

"Thank you. I didn't know you were showing people pictures of me, Bruce."

"Well, the picture slipped out of my wallet," he admitted.

"Yeah, right," I replied.

"Rob, are we ready to go?" Bruce asked while he motioned for us to walk to the back of the building.

"Yes, you are. I just had the guys in maintenance give the car a tune-up, oil change, wash, and a fresh coat of wax. Izzy, congratulations, you're the proud owner of an ocean blue four door Nissan Sentra courtesy of your boyfriend here," Rob explained as he handled me the car keys.

"What?"

"Yes, baby, I bought you a car. You deserve it and you need it. Lord knows, I get tired of trotting you everywhere."

"Thank you so much," I replied with a hug and a long-lasting kiss.

"It's all in a day's work of the Almighty Bruce," he

said, punching his chest. I started walking faster so I could see the car.

After we got outside, I was in awe because of the car. Plus, no one has ever done anything like this for me. It had a leather interior, tape cassette, air conditioner, heat, and huge speakers so I could blast my music.

"Our next stop is going to be Allstate because you need car insurance. I'm going to pay it up for two years. Then, let's go pick up some groceries."

"I can cook you dinner and I'll be the dessert," I cooed.

"Not tonight, I got a few things to take care of. Go home, your momma is probably worried sick about you. Plus, I know you can't wait to tell—no, excuse me—*show* your friends your new car."

"All right," I said with a touch of disappointment. It really meant he needed to do something and I couldn't tag along. I hated being away from him.

Chapter 11

"Isabel Preston, there's always the spring semester when you can start college. I've been holding off the colleges for as long as I can. They need to know an answer," Mom pleaded as I concentrated on packing my belongings. *I might as well take everything,* I thought.

"Mom, as I've been telling you over and over again, I'm not going to college. You can tell the admissions department of each school the same. School isn't for everybody and definitely not for me."

"Bruce and his lifestyle have made you lazy, honey," Grandma Elaine added as she held a dishcloth in her hand.

"I'll agree to that," Mom seconded the notion.

"I'm just taking a break, right now. Finding out what I am meant to do on this earth is hard work. I've got to do a lot of soul-searching." Not working and not going to school was the best plan for my future.

"Do it in college. Bruce is just going to use you and bring you down. Listen to me, baby. I don't want to see you behind a jail cell because you're taking a sentence for him. Put your efforts in yourself and not a man whose time is ticking to end up in jail or dead," Mom demanded.

"My mind is made up. I'm moving in with Bruce. It's the best for all of us. This way, I won't be disrespecting your house by coming in late or not even at all." *Well, this is everything. My life in three suitcases, I thought. There was no need to take lamps, furniture, beds or pillowcases. Bruce will have me well taken care of. Not only was he was my man and best friend, he was a father figure for me. He filled the void that my own daddy left wide open. All I wanted was to be loved.*

"Girl, you're not going anywhere," Mom announced while barricading my bedroom door.

"What are you going to do to stop me? I'm eighteen years old. I can do whatever I want, however I please," I announced.

"I'm forbidding you to leave."

"Whatever! Get out of the way, Mom. Since he's no longer welcome in the house, Bruce is waiting for me in the car for me."

"I bet he can make you even kill for him. All he has to do is open his mouth and you're at his mercy. I never thought the day would come where my own daughter would be pathetic," she spat at me while we were looking into each other's eyes.

"At least you can give Bruce credit for being right by my side. Pathetic, you're one to talk! All these years, you continue to wait for a coward for a husband and a deadbeat daddy. You're weak and I lose respect for you each day. Face it, Daddy doesn't want me and he definitely doesn't want you." Before I could get another word out, Mom slapped me as hard as she could on the left side of my face. I pushed her so hard that she landed on the floor and made my way out of the bedroom.

"Izzy, I'm sorry. Please forgive me," Mom begged as she followed me down the stairs.

"Let her go," Grandma Elaine whispered. I didn't look back at both of them because I didn't want to give Mom the satisfaction of seeing tears of hurt and pain streaming down my face.

"You want to be grown, go on and be grown. Since you're leaving, don't even think about coming back here as long as you're with that man," Mom proclaimed as I walked closer to the car.

Christmastime is fast approaching. At Record Town, I picked Motown's and Luther Vandross's Christmas cassette tapes. I made a quick stop at Kmart to pick up all the trimmings and a tree to make this holiday special for Bruce and me. We were going to make our own memories. This time last year, I was helping Grandma prepare for the annual Christmas dinner. I had to admit I was a little sad about not seeing my family for the holidays. It's been a month since I left Mom's house and haven't seen or heard from her since. Vera and Rachel arrived back home from college yesterday. I talked to each one of them at least twice a week. They weren't in total agreement with us moving in together but at the same time, they felt as though I was an adult and could make my own decisions. Alicia and I have drifted apart. In fact, she's been distant with all of us. The girls are coming to the apartment to help me finish up the holiday decorations. I had prepared Nestlé hot cocoa with marshmallows. The temperature was at a record low of seventeen degrees. The doorbell rang.

"Hey," I said as I hugged Rachel and Vera.

"Merry Christmas," they said in unison as I took their coats. Rachel had a bottle of Bacardi rum in her hand. She was ready to get the night started off right. I quickly got out the glasses. *We can drink the cocoa later,* I thought.

"To friendship and happiness," I suggested.

"To love and big dicks," Rachel added.

"To good grades and well-paying jobs," Vera declared as we toasted.

Two hours passed as we talked about their lives on college campuses. I talked about the drama between Mom and me. Vera and Rachel encouraged me to make amends with her.

"She's the only momma you got, Izzy," Vera proclaimed. Deep down, I was still too angry and hurt all these years to face her. The doorbell rang.

"Hey, where's the party at!" Alicia said as she stepped through the door. Vera, Rachel, and I looked at her in disbelief. Six months ago, Alicia was severely overweight. At times, she even had problems breathing to do normal activities. For example, going up and down a staircase or bending over to tie her sneakers would cause problems. Now, standing before us was her at least sixty pounds lighter. Damn, the girl was skin and bones. Plus, the leather skirt she had on was barely covering her butt cheeks. She never dressed like that before. Now she could and was flaunting it.

"Ah, I see the way you all are looking at me. I've been working out heavily. Girls, I had to get it off," Alicia explained. As we huddled in the living room, she started telling us how she lost the weight and how school was going. Before I knew it, Bruce walked in.

"Hey, baby," I greeted with a kiss. "This is Alicia, Vera, and Rachel."

"Girls, this is my man and baby-boo, Bruce," I giggled. He shook each of the girls' hand and made eye contact with Vera and Rachel but not Alicia.

"Guess what?" Alicia announced with excitement.

"What?" we all responded in unison.

"Our favorite store, Merry Go Round in Military Circle

Mall is having a fifty-percent off sale. We should go. Nowadays I love going shopping. Let's go to the mall before it closes. Plus, I need a new outfit so we can go to the new hot spot, Boombox," she suggested, sliding her hands down her hips.

"Let's go, I'll drive," Vera responded, getting our coats out of the hall closet.

"It was nice meeting you, ladies. Before you go, Izzy, can I see you in the bedroom, please?" he said, walking down the hall.

"Sure; ya'll, I'll be right back," I explained as they put on their hats and scarfs.

"Yes, baby?" I asked as Bruce closed the door once I entered.

"What the hell are you doing bringing your friends up in my place?" he whispered in my ear as he slapped my face with the back of his hand.

"I thought this was our place together?" I whimpered.

"Don't get it twisted. You don't pay no bills here. I can and will throw you out whenever I see fit. Your friends cannot come here no more. The only three people that can cross that door is me, you, and my best friend, Theo. Understand?" he demanded.

"I get it. You never told me no one was welcome," I replied, almost in tears, cupping my hands to my stinging face. I ran to the bathroom to apply a hot washcloth on my face. It didn't look that bad. Bruce and I got into a fight about two weeks ago because I stayed at the department store too long. I tried to explain that JCPenney's was swarming with people but he didn't want to hear it and slammed me up against the wall. I had to soak in a hot bath for three days to get some relief from the soreness. Now, I'm slowly realizing what Mom and Grandma were saying to me all these years: based on the choices that I make, I will suffer the consequences. What's next for me, a broken jaw or rib? Worst of all, I deserved it even more if I stay. Giving up this life of luxury will be hard. Besides, my ass beating doesn't as nearly hurt as working a full eight-hour day. Grandma was right about another thing, I am getting lazy.

I grabbed my bags and planned to leave Bruce, but after a gold chain, one-karat pear-shaped diamond earrings, his promise he wouldn't do it ever again, and his willingness to consider counseling, I decided to stick this relationship out with him. Growing up, Bruce's step-father beat on his mother. I guess old habits are hard to break. I love him and he doesn't mean to get so angry. Everyone deserves another chance.

"Izzy, you ain't seen no one else come in this apartment. You know what I do to get these bills paid on time every month. Use your head and stop being so fucking stupid. I'm going to take a hot shower. What's for dinner? I'm tired and had a long day. Plus, I have to leave back out tonight."

"I cooked spaghetti with meatballs. I put a plate in the refrigerator for you," I said, starting the water for him as he went into the walk-in closet. Then, I grabbed a bottle of laxative tablets and tucked it in my pocket.

"Look, I left four hundred dollars on the bed for you and your girls. Sorry for roughing you up. Have a good time. Don't wait up for me," he said, taking off his Nautica sweatshirt. Bruce had come from playing basketball. The smell of sweat filled the bathroom.

"Girls, give me ten minutes. Go ahead to the car, I'll be right down." As soon as I heard Bruce step into the shower, I quickly went into action, taking his plate out of the refrigerator. I took out about five tablets and ground them into a white powder. I quickly sprinkled the medicine on top of the dinner and mixed it all together. When the white laxative dissolved into the spaghetti, I put the plate back into the refrigerator, almost forgetting to pour the cocoa down in a jar and place the cups into the dishwasher. Not too long ago, Grandma gave it to me when I couldn't have a bowel movement. When given in big doses, you have no choice but to be glued to the toilet. Not to mention, it causes severe cramping. Bruce wasn't going anywhere tonight but the bathroom. It's going to be a long night for him. As he huddles over the toilet, maybe he'll think putting his hands on me isn't such a good idea.

"Bye, baby," I yelled as I headed toward the door. Bruce ignored me because he was too busy singing the shower.

Vera and Rachel rode with me while Alicia insisted that she drive her own car.

"Ladies, I have something to tell you," I suggested while driving to the mall and Alicia was behind me.

"Izzy, what is it?" Vera asked.

"Well, Alicia's mother called me last week and told me that she has been using heroin."

"What!" Rachel blurt out.

"What happened to make her turn to drugs?" Vera questioned.

"A few girls are influencing and using her at the university. Alicia spends all her money that her parents send her for books and expenses on drugs. Her mother also thinks she's using it to lose weight. She only sees Alicia when she wants money. She found the drugs in one of her bedroom drawers."

"This is horrible," Rachel whimpered with tears coming down her eyes.

"What are we going to do?" Vera questioned.

"I don't know. Her mother wants us to talk to her about getting help but I'm afraid to say something because she might get defensive. Let's just see if she brings it up to us. Whatever you do, don't give her ass any money. We don't want to become enablers, as her mother has requested."

"Alicia's mother does enough enabling for the three of us." Vera said.

"Did ya'll notice Bruce didn't speak to her at the apartment?" I mentioned.

"Yeah, I did notice that, myself," Vera added.

"Well, I think she might have bought from him. You know? What else would be the reason that he wouldn't look at her or speak to her?" I asked them to wonder over.

"Bruce loves you. I hope Alicia isn't trying to take him away. I don't know what you would do to her, Izzy," Vera blurted out.

"Alicia wouldn't dare cross me," I replied.

"Hopefully, she will check herself into a drug rehab center. She looks awful," Rachel broadcasted.

We spent an hour at the Merry Go Round. At Bruce's request, I got each of them an outfit. It was an early Christmas gift. Later on, we decided to eat at the Golden Wok in the food court. Everyone ordered food except Alicia. Her whole demeanor had changed once we arrived at the mall.

"Alicia, are you sure you don't want anything?" I offered for the third time.

"Food is the last thing in my mind. I'm fine, girl," she insisted.

"All right," I replied, shrugging my shoulders.

"I do have a small confession to make," Alicia suggested.

"I'm listening," I answered, wondering what she was going to say.

"Let's wait for Vera and Rachel to finish ordering because I'm only going to say it once because I know you will tell them what's going on."

"Okay," I suggested, waiting eagerly for her response.

"What's going on?" Vera asked while putting her tray down on the table, noticing Alicia's puzzled face.

"Izzy, there's one thing you should know."

"What's that?" I asked.

"Your man used to be mine. We dated for two years. He is one of the biggest drug lords in the Tidewater area. Men fear him and women wish they could get a taste of him. All I'm saying is be careful. I would hate for you to get caught into something. Plus, by the way Bruce was staring at me, I don't think he's over our relationship. I'm sure you noticed he spoke to Vera and Rachel but not me," she explained. I didn't know what to think and I had lost my appetite. *Could she be lying and just trying to get me out of the way to get more drugs out of Bruce? Before I get my ass beat again, I had to be careful as how I would approach him,* I thought. After shopping, Alicia had an appointment that just couldn't wait. She gave all of us hugs and exited her way out of the mall.

Chapter 12

As I predicted, Bruce's car was still in the complex parking lot. Marching up the stairs, I was filled with confidence. There's no way he would figure out I had laced his spaghetti with that powerful laxative cocktail. When I got to the mall, I threw the bottle away in the trash can. Although I wanted him to pay for the lying and abuse, I was secretly hoping I didn't erupt one of his intestines with all of the medication.

"Izzy, baby is that you?" Bruce asked. His voice was weak coming from behind the bathroom door.

"Yes," I replied, opening the bathroom door.

"Since you left, I had the runs all night. I couldn't even leave out. I think it was those mangoes I bought today from the store. My stomach is tore up. I'm scared to leave the toilet. You know I can't have shit drippings on the carpet," he said, hovered over the toilet, rocking back and forth.

"So when were you going to tell me that you knew Alicia?"

"I see she beat me to it."

"How long were you two an item?" I asked as he had the bathroom door cracked open.

"What are you talking about?"

"Alicia said you two were together," I explained.

"Alicia and I were never together. All she did was suck my dick to pay for her drugs. I used a condom, of course. Watch out for that girl. She's no good. Those drugs changed her. Listen, Izzy, I was going to tell you in time. I have to admit when I first met you, I didn't know if we were going to last or not. I'm not proud of what I do. Eventually, I will stop and lead a normal life. For now, pulling six thousand a day is hard to leave."

"I can't believe you did something with Alicia!" I said in shock, completly ignoring the last part of what he said.

"I'm sorry, but Izzy, it goes with the territory. Alicia couldn't pay with money so she did by other ways. Alicia probably might have figured that you would leave me after hearing her lies. You can't go off the deep end on me because I didn't know she was your friend until tonight. *He had a point but I wasn't going to show it,* I thought.

"That girl is either using drugs most of the time or bending over to supply her habit. Deep down, Alicia is wishing to be my girl. No lie," he explained, holding his hands up.

"I hope she will stop and get help soon," I added.

"Maybe she will for her sake," Bruce stated.

I turned on the stereo in our bedroom. "Freak Me" by Silk was playing on the *Midnight Storm* on 103 JAMZ. I did a sensational striptease for Bruce in the hallway. He loved it when I bounced my ass in his face. He loved my ass more than my titties. One of them landed in his mouth. I continued to jiggle them in his face.

"My dick is getting hard, Izzy. I'm going fuck you up against the wall."

"You can do whatever you want to me once you get tested for crabs, chlamydia, gonorrhea, syphilis, and AIDS. We haven't ever used condoms. I don't know who your nasty ass has been with," I announced.

Grabbing only two outfits and only grabbing two fistfuls of panties, bras, and socks, I headed to the door, knowing Grandma Elaine would let me stay with her. There was no way I was going back to Mom's house. I vowed never to speak another word of this to Vera, Rachel or Alicia. It was all too awkward for me. Some things should be left alone, especially if the girl may try to get herself back on track.

Since I'd moved into this apartment, I've been waiting on Bruce hand and foot with him having a fit if I leave the apartment. Bruce is very controlling and I hope he will change his ways. For example, when we watch television he has to hold the remote and we never watch what I want. In addition, he always has to get in the shower first, leaving me with a speck of hot water. I have to wait thirty minutes for the water to warm back up again. Even the little controlling things he does are getting under my skin. At times, I feel more of a prisoner than a girlfriend. Cooking, cleaning, washing clothes, and counting endless straps of money. Once the money is counted and strapped, I store it in the closet of our spare bedroom. To make it easier on me, I suggested to him that he invest in two money counters. After two weeks, he caved in and brought them to the apartment. Now, I needed a break.

Chapter 13

Bruce and I got tested together for every sexually transmitted disease known to man and AIDS. As a result, we were both found negative going into the New Year. I convinced him that I couldn't stay on birth control anymore because it made me very nauseous so we had to use condoms. Little did he know, it was just a precaution for now and I continued to take my little yellow pills. To celebrate, he whisked me away on a two-week vacation to Key West in Florida for fun and relaxation. Life couldn't be any better. Bruce and I were at the hotel bar. He was drinking a Heineken while I was sipping on a raspberry daiquiri. Bruce had a fake ID made so I could drink. I'm one more year from being twenty-one years old. Most bartenders were skeptical but went along, giving me the drink. Plus, he spared no expense when we were out. Bruce was the type of guy who loved to flash his money and wanted anyone who would listen to know. Some nights he wouldn't go to sleep but end up looking out the window with his bottle of whiskey in the left hand and his AK-47 in the right hand. *What a way I live*, I thought, getting up to use the bathroom and then going back to sleep.

"Izzy, I'm going to get out of this life. I can't do it anymore," Bruce announced while smoking on a Cuban cigar.

"Why the sudden change?" I asked with a hint of happiness in my voice. Sure, I believed him that he wanted to stop, but actions speak louder than words. If he stopped, does that mean my money train stops too? It's been a while and I'm not getting another job.

"In three more years, I'll be thirty. What do I got to show for it but beating jail time and court cases? I'm realizing there's more to me than the drug life. The money I have put up I may want to open a service center for cars. You know, people can slide through and get oil changes, car washes, tune-ups, new tires, tire rotations, and whatever else I can do to maintenance a car."

"It sounds like a plan and I'll help you any way I can," I tried to convince him, rubbing his shoulders. Just as long as the money doesn't run out. This is Bruce's fault; he made me this way and I have no plans to change.

"Oh, by the way, happy birthday, Izzy," he mentioned while he slid a Tiffany box and another box my way. Tiffany had to be opened first. Inside were diamond hoops. I preferred diamonds more than gold because it was shinier. When we get back to Virginia, I made a mental note to open a safety deposit box to store all this jewelry I had and would probably be getting in the future. Next, inside the second box was a picture of Vera, Rachel, Alicia, and I at our first year at camp. Tears streamed down my face.

"Thank you, Bruce. I love the picture and the earrings," I insisted while putting them on and admiring the picture.

"You're welcome. Pick your lip up. Izzy, I didn't want to make you cry. I had the picture blown up. I know you miss your friends while they're away at school. Cell phones just came out and I know they're expensive. My man, Harvin at RadioShack, can work a deal out with me where both of us can get a phone. This way, you can talk to your friends and I can handle my business."

"You would do that for me, baby?"

"Of course. Now, dry up those tears. We're going to an exclusive restaurant called Trilogy and I want to have hot sex till my dick starts hurting when we get back to the hotel."

"Don't want to hurt you."

"Try me," he stated, running his fingers in the back of my right ear down to my neck.

Chapter 14

Bruce had me counting moneys from sunup to sundown. I was beginning to get small blisters on my hands. One-hundred-dollar bills and fifty-dollar bills must be hand counted, according to him. He was becoming more of a tyrant and less of a boyfriend. He was in the mood for salmon and I had almost two hours before he got home to prepare it. After thirty more minutes, I ran to Farm Fresh to pick up wild rice and fresh-cut broccoli. Today was gloomy, rainy, and traffic was horrible. On the way home, I was stuck at the stoplight for an hour because there was a six-car pileup in front of me. Worst of all, I had to pee.

As I turned the key of the front door, I was soaked from the rain but sizzling in irritation from my schedule being sidetracked. To my surprise, Bruce was all ready home.

"Izzy, I thought you were going to have dinner made already? I'm starving. Girl, you know I can't keep eating fast food every day of my life," he screamed.

"You're home almost an hour early," I replied, looking at the time on the microwave. Next thing, Bruce came from behind and pinned me down to the kitchen floor, knocking the grocery bag out of my hand. Bits of broccoli splattered all over the floor.

"All I ask of you is a decent meal and that you hand count fifty- and one-hundred-dollar bills. Ones, fives, tens, and twenty-dollar bills, you just run through the machine. How hard is that, Izzy?" he stated, holding my right arm in a tight grip. It hurt to breathe. *He's going to break my arm*, I thought.

"The rain caused major traffic on the streets. There was a terrible accident," I whimpered with tears in my eyes.

"You always got a damn excuse."

"Please, let my arm go. I'll fix you whatever you want."

"Oh, I know that, but first please tell me why one hundred bills are sitting in the money counter."

"I—"

"Don't want to see it again," he stated, cutting me off. "Now, fix me something to eat," he demanded while kneeing me in the stomach. Then, his cell phone rang.

"Baby, I need to take this call outside," he said, helping me up from the kitchen floor and giving me a kiss on the cheek. I could barely stand up. In an instant, Bruce can go from a tyrant to a sweet, loving guy. Each time he hit me I could hear Mom telling me I would reap what I sow for the choices that I make. I'm paying a high price. The rate I'm going, I wonder if I'll have to pay with my life for living the drug life? Not only do I have to take Bruce's beatings but also look over my shoulder and wonder if anyone else wants me dead to retaliate on him. As soon as he walked out of the door, I managed to place a chair from the dinette set under the front door. Next, I called

Theo, his best friend and explained to him what happened. He was more interested in getting me to a hospital than dealing with Bruce. I was going to be all right as long as the tyrant didn't come back for any more licks to add to my body.

Chapter 15

The walls were caving down on me. It's been four days since I've seen Bruce. He's banged on the door countless times but I won't let him in. Five more days go by, my bruises have gone away, and I'm starting to miss my man. I take the chair away from the door. Around eight o'clock that night, Bruce comes strolling in. As he hangs up his coat in the closet, I began to realize I was falling out of love with him. With each of his blows resulting in a black eye, slap—and his ultimate favorite, the kick—more of my love was fading away just like my bruises. Time would only tell if this man who I once adored would kill me. Bruce didn't show up empty-handed. Peach roses and a mixed light brown and dark brown fur coat came with him. This was all routine for him and me. Tomorrow, I'll be back at that kitchen table counting money as if nothing ever happened.

We watched the popular television show *Martin*. Then I went to the bedroom to go to bed. To be honest, I never could get good rest unless the tyrant wasn't here. I took off my clothes and noticed in the mirror there's still a slight bruise where he kicked me in the stomach.

"I'm sorry." Bruce entered, kneeling down by my side, clutching my hips. I didn't respond but just stood there. We began to cry together.

"You need help with your anger. Bruce, what if you would have broken one of my ribs?"

"I'm going to get help. I promise."

"We can even go together," I added, hoping there was a shred of truth in him wanting to go to counseling. I kneeled beside him as we held each other for fifteen minutes. He ripped off my banana-striped thongs and instantly started sucking my clitoris.

"No, stop," I insisted, trying to move his head away from my pussy.

"Hmm, hmm," he responded with his head still nudged between my legs, licking my clitoris hard, back and forth with his tongue. Bruce's hands were gripped on my breasts with his fingers flicking my hard nipples. I came so hard I shivered in heartache of the man who I loved but beat me and the desire of this man to get his temper under control. Deep down, I had to come up with a plan to leave 1524 Cunning Place, Apartment 105 permanently.

Chapter 16

Five months had passed and Bruce hadn't laid a finger on me since. Any extra money I got from him I took to the safety deposit at the nearest local bank to hold for a day that I would need it. These days, I was looking forward to Bruce coming home. We started played board games such as chess, Scrabble, and Monopoly. He wasn't the hanging-in-the-club-every-night guy, which I was grateful for. Both of us were very competitive. Tonight, I'd prepared smothered pork chops, black eyes marinated in country ham, and sweet corn on the cob. All those years sitting around the kitchen with Grandma Elaine paid off. For dessert, I picked up a few cannolis from the pastry shop on Newtown Road.

"Dinner hit the spot tonight," Bruce said, rubbing his stomach and putting back on his white Reebok classics.

"Where are you going? It's game night. I've got the kettle popcorn and Fanta peach soda ready to go," I stated.

"Not tonight, I've got to pick up Theo's slack. He's on vacation in Los Angeles, remember."

"Oh yeah. Well, let me go with you. We haven't been out in months, please."

"Nah, Izzy, where I pick up my money isn't a place for you."

"I'm curious to see." I persuaded him while unbuttoning his jeans and pulling out his dick from his gray boxers. I loved to suck his dick while he was standing up. Bruce tried so hard not to fall to his knees. He loved it when I deep-throated him. One thing I don't do is swallow a man's cum. Vera and Rachel told me that it makes your stomach hurt.

Chapter 17

"When we get in here, don't talk to anyone. I got a bad feeling letting you in one of my crack houses. I don't want to expose you to this world. Here's a twenty-two caliber, just in case somebody wants to act funny. Once we're in, go the back room and pick up the brown paper bag by the lamp. Whatever you do, don't go upstairs. I want to be able to keep an eye on you," he explained, handing me the gun. It wasn't too heavy.

"I promise to follow behind you," I assured him. Before entering, one lady with no teeth and smelled as if she hadn't washed herself in a week was willing to sell her baby's diapers just for a hit. He refused and I was proud of him.

Once inside, there were scrawny people at the door in a trancelike state. They looked like zombies. The smell was so foul I almost vomited. We were greeted by two of Bruce's street soldiers selling the drugs inside the home. The process was simple. A person bangs on the door and you have to say the correct password. If the potential consumer didn't look right or if you got a bad vibe, they weren't given anything. Bruce and Theo liked to put the money earned each day in safes in different locations of this house just in case they got robbed; at least one stash could be salvaged. Each safe was buried under the hardwood floor. One man was banging his head against the wall. Some were simply sitting on the steps. This once probably was a lovely two-story home. Bruce told me it had been abandoned. He and Theo set up shop.

"Izzy, stop staring and go get the money. I want to get you outta here as soon as possible," he instructed. I went to the back room and heard voices. Bruce said no one should ever be in the back room.

"Bruce, there's someone in there," I relayed back to him.

"Well, let's see what's going on in that room," Bruce proclaimed with his gun clutched tightly. He kicked the door only for me to discover my father, a man, and another woman stumbling to put their clothes on. My father has been strung out on crack cocaine this whole time and Mom never bothered to tell me. Why? Was she trying to shelter me from all this hurt and pain? How long has he been on drugs? Did my mother really know? Is my father a homosexual? Many questions were racing through my mind.

"Daddy," I called out. He didn't even recognize me or even realize I was standing right in front of him. I guess he was so high from the drugs it was clouding his judgment. I threw the lamp at him and he fell to the floor. All of my anger, hurt, and frustration had come to a head. Daddy left us for drugs and this kind of dead-end lifestyle. I ran out of the house as quickly as I could, forgetting to pick up the paper bag filled with money. Bruce followed my trail but stopped to remind his street soldiers no one was allowed in the back room. He remembered to pick up the bag.

Chapter 18

"Girl, why did you run out like that?" Bruce asked.
"The man . . ."

"Did he hurt you? If so, he will get dealt with," he ordered, cutting me off.

"That man is my father. I haven't heard or seen him in almost ten years. Daddy stopped caring for me and my mother," I said, crying profusely, almost in a state of shock.

"Isabel, I'm so sorry you had to see your father like this. I knew I shouldn't have brought you out here, tonight. Damn, I feel so fucking guilty," he whispered while hugging me.

"How long has Daddy been coming in here?"

"You don't want to know," he responded, shaking his head.

"Please, please, tell me."

"About seven years, I've seen your pops on and off. On when he had money and off when his money was scarce."

"He didn't even recognize me."

"Try not to take it personal, crack clouds your judgement. Out of all my crack houses, I will send out a direct order for my people not to accept money from your father or allow him in. To be honest, there are plenty of other crack houses, so this measure I'm taking will only slow him down for so long."

"Thank you."

"Do you want to go home to see and talk with your mother? I understand if you need to go."

"No, I just want to go back to *our* home," I whimpered, burying my head into his chest.

Chapter 19

In the car, I couldn't stop crying. A part of me was infuriated about what I discovered about my father. From this day forth, he doesn't deserve to be called Daddy. Another part of me was relieved to finally know the truth about all these years. Once we arrived home, Bruce whipped up a mug of hot chocolate with three marshmallows and a touch of cinnamon, just the way I like it.

"Izzy, I think you should go talk to your mother about tonight," he suggested. Hmm, he's one to talk. Two days after the funeral of his brother, Bruce moved out his mother's house and refused any contact with her since. He blames her for killing Timothy.

"No, I don't feel like talking to her right now. If I did want to talk to Mom, she would probably be more concerned about how Daddy looked than my physical and emotional well-being. My head is pounding. Can you get me the bottle of Motrin out of the medicine cabinet?" I asked while rubbing my temples together.

"Coming right up," he insisted.

"Thank you," I whimpered.

"Look at me, green eyes," Bruce ordered after giving me the pills.

"Yes?" I responded after taking them. *My green eyes are probably bloodshot with all that crying I just did.*

"I will promise to never, ever leave your side as your father did," Bruce vowed.

"Thank you."

After a hot bath, Bruce gave me a one-hour massage. He made sweet love to me, making sure I felt every of inch of his eight-inch dick. Tonight, we decided not to use a condom. I wanted to be as close to him as I could.

Chapter 20

Looking at the time on my cell phone, it read two o'clock in the morning. Bruce, Theo, Rena (Theo's girlfriend), and I were enjoying an evening at the club Dazzle on Granby Street. Rena called it a night one hour ago and drove home. After four rum and Cokes, I was a little tipsy myself. The lights came on and the club owner got onstage.

"Thanks for another Saturday night. The club is officially closed. You don't got to go home but you got to get the hell up outta here. Folks, please don't forget next door is my soul food restaurant, Mabel's. Stop by and grab a bite to eat. For the next three hours, we have the early-bird special where plates are twenty-five off regular price," he announced on the mic.

The Waffle House on Indian River Road is where Bruce and I were headed to.

* * *

"Izzy, there has been a change of plans. I have to go take care of something right now," Bruce insisted.

"Where are—?"

"Ask questions later. I need to go. Theo is going to drive you home. He's waiting for you outside," he instructed, cutting me off and giving me a kiss on the lips. Bruce drowned in the sea of people leaving the building, all headed in the same direction. There's one way in and one way out.

Theo was drunk himself and I prayed that we didn't hit another vehicle or a pole. He continued to swerve in and out of lanes.

"Thank you for the ride," I said, relieved I had made it home in one place.

"Sorry about my driving. Maybe I had one too many Heinekens," Theo admitted.

"It's all right. Next time, I know not to get in the car with you. Good night," I replied, unlocking the passenger-side door of his silver Lexus.

"Izzy, do you mind if I use the bathroom? I've got to pee."

"Sure, come on in."

"I appreciate you letting me use the bathroom. A weight has been lifted off. Now, I need to sober up. Do you have Coca-Cola in the refrigerator?" Theo asked.

"Yes, can you pour me a glass of soda too?" I asked while flipping through the channels of the television in the living room.

"Of course."

"This will help me too," I said before drinking the last bit of soda in my glass.

"I prefer Coca-Cola over Sprite to get me through hangovers." Suddenly, I started to feel queasy. The room was spinning out of control as I tried to get up from the couch. "Theo, take me to the hospital. I don't feel right," I whispered. *I will never drink again.*

"Lie down," he insisted, motioning my body back on the couch. Theo started taking off my Sergio Valente jeans.

"Theo, what are you doing?" I asked, trying to move to pull my jeans backs up.

"Ssh, relax, you won't remember a thing in the morning." It only took a second of sober thinking to realize that I had been drugged.

"Bruce has the life, the apartment, more money and power than me. I just live in his shadow. More importantly, he's got you and your Coca-Cola glass-bottle figure," he explained while licking my left thigh. Then, he pulled my black G-string down to my ankles. Next, he unbuckled his belt and pulled out his dick.

"Please, Theo, what about Rena?" I asked, barely getting out the words.

"What about her? I don't love her ass. It's you I want. Isabel, I love you. Give me a taste of your pussy. Bruce doesn't deserve you. You try your best to cover up those bruises but I know what's going on. His temper is out of control and your body suffers from it."

"No, Theo, don't do this," I begged, not being able to move at this point.

"It has to be done, but I will use a condom. You can't have my baby like this," he proclaimed, spreading my legs and placing the condom on. His dick entered into my pussy.

"Stop, you're hurting me."

"Don't worry, Izzy, I come fast." Theo penetrated me at least eight or nine times.

"I'm about to come," he announced. I was beginning to lose count.

I heard the door crack open. Bruce came in the house in disbelief. He threw Theo off of me and started beating him with the butt of his 9 mm. I blacked out.

When I finally came to, Bruce was in the reclining chair by the bed. He looked at me and got up from the chair to gently rub my hair. I felt as if I had slept for two days. The clock read six o'clock in the evening. I heard voices outside of the door.

"Hey, baby," he whimpered.

"What happened?" I asked.

"Izzy, listen, because we will never have this conversation again. You can't tell a soul what happened here. First of all, I'm getting out of the drug life. We're moving to a new apartment. I broke the lease here and settled a deal with the office manager. The new complex is called Columbus Station near Pembroke Mall. It's in a quiet neighborhood. I need to lay low for a while. I thought Theo was my friend. Hell, he was a brother to me. Where you could find me, you could find him. I didn't realize how jealous he can become of me. We started this business together. It's not my fault he ventured into business opportunities that didn't go anywhere and made him lose large sums of money. One of the safes was missing fifty thousand dollars. He admitted everything to me. Theo put a drug called 'roofies' in your soda. It damn near paralyzed you. I almost took you to the hospital. Once I saw you were breathing, I gave you a hot bath and and put you in the bed. Before putting you in the tub, I even used a bottle of that douche stuff I always see you using, hoping it would clean you out *up* there. I'm so sorry this has happened to you. I don't understand how he could rape you! Izzy, you of all people! I thought he looked at you as a little sister. Instead, he sat there plotting to make a move on you. He was the one who said I had to go pick up the money last night because he wanted to get to Rena's house early. I killed him and he deserved to die. The boys and I took him to the butcher shop and cut him up. I have a present for you," he explained, holding up a white cloth. Inside were Theo's thumb and his right ear. A chill went down my spine.

"Your favorite, *stromboli* from Primo Pizza with extra tomato sauce is sitting in the refrigerator for you. I got some loose ends to tie up. I'll be back in a couple of hours. Are you going to be all right?" he asked while rolling the ear and thumb back into the white cloth. Then he put it into his left coat pocket.

"Yes, please hurry back. Could you do one thing for me?" I questioned.

"Anything."

"Throw out all of the Coca-Cola in the refrigerator."

Chapter 21

Four years had gone by. Neither Bruce nor I have saved much money. In the beginning, I did but then got too caught up in jewelry, Gucci, Versace, and Armani. He did get rid of the drug life; however, now he's acquired a taste for robbing banks, which could get him twenty-to-life no matter if he steals a dollar or a million dollars. His crew and him wear masks to hide their faces during all five of the robberies. When were they going to stop? Each one was done outside of the Hampton Roads area of Virginia. Bruce would travel as far as Petersburg, Roanoke, and Alexandria. It's just a matter of time before he gets caught. It was difficult for Bruce and I to start having sex again. Both of us were traumatized from the rape. Now, we never used condoms. I'm staring at myself in the mirror. The mirror is staring back at a young girl whose left eye is swollen from the slap of Bruce's back hand. I forgot to lock the sliding glass door last night and this is what I received in return. I deserve every bit of this. I've wasted six years of my life and all I got to show for it is jewelry and designer clothes. Now, I can't live like this, something has got to change. I want to leave him but I'm not trying to get a job. Being accustomed to waking up at ten o'clock every morning is a hard habit to break.

I had to admit Bruce was right about Alicia. She dropped out of school and is a full-time heroin addict. Her parents intervened but Alicia refuses to get help. This has practically broken her mother's heart. She would give away a kidney just to get a hit. Over the years, she's been hitting me up for a one-hundred- and two-hundred-dollars loans. Finally, I wised up and told her I didn't have the money and that's when I didn't see her anymore. Now, I know where to find her. She's on Church Street selling her body to get what she craves. Vera and Rachel graduated from college. Vera is a vice president of an insurance claims department and Rachel works as a mortgage loan officer at BankFIRST. What the hell do I have to show for the past years? Let's see: a broken jaw, twenty stitches, fifty bruises, eight black eyes, and two broken ribs.

Realizing life is too short, I'm trying to amend my relationship with Mom. When Bruce is out of town, I will go spend those nights at her house. I still haven't told her about seeing my father in the crack house. My anger and hurt won't let me ponder where he's at or if he's even still alive.

Next week, Grandma Elaine will be honored at Core Street Baptist Church for being a member for fifty years. Mom has begged me to come. Bruce is tagging along in support, as well.

Chapter 22

Bruce and I got dressed up in our finest clothing to go to Grandma Elaine's church event. He put on an Issey Miyake dark gray suit and I wore a Ann Taylor black pantssuit. The whole congregation showed up to honor my grandmother. I didn't want to but I sat in the first row with her. Little did she know, I slipped a card with an envelope containing a thousand dollars in her purse. A portion of Bruce's blood money must go to good use. During the ceremony, they showed many pictures of her during church events over the years. The pastor and associate Pastor Ruff thanked her for being a faithful servant of the Lord.

The church ladies had prepared a feast down in the basement for us to enjoy. As everyone assembled downstairs, I was getting hungry from the sweet aroma. Three tables were laid out with food. There was turkey, baked chicken, fried chicken, roasted pig, baked fish, fried fish, and country ham. The second table consisted of two trays of macaroni and cheese. I knew that would go fast. Also, it had collard greens, corn on the cob, string beans, lima beans, black-eyed peas, broccoli and cheese casserole, fresh-baked white and wheat rolls, and sweet cornbread. The third table consisted of punch, sodas, sweet and unsweetened tea, and water. In addition, fresh bread pudding, vanilla cake, peach, raspberry, and apple-crumb cobbler, chocolate cake, puff pastries, sugar cookies, and chocolate éclairs lay on the table.

We all bowed our heads for Mom to say grace. *Good, we can all eat,* I thought.

"Umm, before we get started eating, I have an announcement to make," Mom proclaimed, walking toward the door. None other than my father in a brown suit appeared in the basement. "Everyone, this is my husband, Shawn Preston." *He look as if he's aged a bit but still he had smooth skin and all his teeth were still in place.*

"He's been hooked on crack cocaine for over ten years but today I'm here to tell you God has delivered him from his addiction," Mom proclaimed.

"With the help of a praying wife that never gave up on me, a praying mother-in-law and the power will of myself to stop, I am a renewed man," my father announced.

"Hallejuah, thank you Jesus," a woman's voice cried out. A man's voice started speaking in tongues. These people were moved by a deadbeat and a coward.

"I'm not finished. Shawn and I are renewing our vows and would be honored if the Head Pastor Sears and Pastor Ruff would conduct the ceremony. "Both of them nodded their heads in unison. I bet those two couldn't wait until next Sunday so they could parade my father around as a hero because he wanted to finally get off his ass and get off drugs. Hmm, what a man! The offering will probably double.

"Izzy, baby, Daddy's back," Mom said, walking over to me and holding my hand. I quickly grabbed my hand back from her.

"Wait a minute, you knew he was a crackhead all these years?" I questioned her, looking right into her eyes.

"Yes," she reluctantly replied with her head down.

"Why didn't you tell me? I kept asking you over and over again what was going on with him."

"I didn't want to hurt you. You were too young too understand."

"I understand that I don't have a father. I'm twenty-two years old. When was I going to be old enough to understand? I turned eighteen fours ago, you could have said something then! You told me everything but the truth. He hasn't been there for me since I was in middle school. Do you know many tears I cried on missed birthdays, Christmases, Thanksgivings, Easter, recitals, and Father's Days? Not even a phone call to me, Mom? Why are you taking him back? For years, you struggled because of him. He has caused us so much hurt and pain," I struck back at her.

"I'm a new man, baby," Daddy butted in, reaching to give me a hug.

"Don't you dare touch me," I responded, reaching into my purse to get out my bottle of Mace. I sprayed into his eyes. My father fell to the floor. One of the church ladies ran to get him a warm washcloth.

"Girl, what are you doing?" Mom asked while desperately trying to get the bottle out of my hand.

"Izzy, I know you're upset; please give your mother the bottle," Grandma Elaine begged. People started standing back.

"It's either him or me, Mom," I demanded.

"Give Daddy another chance. He'll make it up to you."

"When I get up from this floor, I'm going . . ." my father said while his hands were clutched to his eyes.

"You're going to what?" I asked, cutting him off. A burst of rage came over me. I punched him in the face and repeatedly kept kicking my father in his back. People were too scared to intervene. Plus, I think some felt he deserved it. Bruce picked me up to get me off of him.

"Calm down, Isabel," Bruce demanded.

"It's either him or me, Mom! Decide right now, who is it going to be?" I asked, almost out of breath, ignoring Bruce.

"Your father and I are staying together whether you like it or not. He's my husband and I love him. I've had to suffer the consequences of loving a man who was a drug addict. He wasn't around and I waited for ten years for him to get his life. I could've moved on but I chose not to. We all make choices and have to pay for them, good or bad, Izzy."

"I'm your daughter and I thought you loved me," I proclaimed with tears in my eyes.

"Baby," Mom reached out.

"I stopped being your baby a long time ago. Mom, I hate you and that piece of trash you call a man," I screamed at the top of my lungs.

As I walked out, I knocked all three of the tables. Now, all the good food was all over the floor.

"This is not a joyous occasion," I announced, walking out of the door with Bruce slowly following behind me. Out of the corner of my eye, I saw him give Pastor Ruff ten crisp, new hundred-dollar bills. I guess to pay for the mess I had made.

Chapter 23

Bruce decided to drive us out to Virginia Beach. We parked the car on Market Avenue between Seventh and Eighth Street. We talked and walked on the boardwalk for what seemed hours. I cried and cried and did some more crying. All these years, I was carrying this pain and anger. It had to be let out. Now, I felt ashamed and embarrassed for disrespecting my grandmother on her day of honor. I didn't know when I could work up the nerve to go and apologize to her. Mom and my nonexistent father, on the other hand, were a different story. My mother chose him over me, which I knew if I had to come to it, she would choose him, hands down. Now I began to wonder if Mom stopped loving me too. Was I so bad as a child? Why did Daddy leave in the first place? Was it drugs at first or maybe another woman? Over the years, I even begged Uncle Ronnie to tell me where my father was. He too couldn't offer any answers for me. Plus, Mom knew he was a crack addict all along and never bothered to tell me face-to-face, mother to daughter, what was going on. Bruce suggested I go get my answers from the source: my father. There was no way my biological parents would lay eyes on me or hear my voice ever again in life. The other person who loved me dearly was Grandma Elaine. All I did was act a fool, on her day. Bruce had the nerve to suggest I needed counseling. He never got the counseling he promised to get five years ago.

Once back at Columbus Station, Bruce gave me a sedative to sleep. Little did I know those pills would become my new best friends.

Chapter 24

Bruce and I were refusing all cell phone calls, which was the only way people could reach us. No one had the house phone number except him and me. Mom and my father starting calling Bruce's cell when I wouldn't pick up. Besides being hurt and alone, I was embarrassed to go out in public. For the next six months, I would be talked about for my outburst. Eventually, I'm going to have to work up the nerve to apologize to Grandma Elaine and the congregation of Core Street Baptist Church. The last time I heard from Grandma was through a voice mail she had left. It took the men and women all night to clean up the mess I made. Vera and Rachel were blowing up my phone too but I didn't feel like talking. All I wanted to do was sleep. Two months have passed and it still hurts as much as the day Mom chose my father over me. I still wasn't taking my mother's calls and she was leaving voice mails on my cell phone.

* * *

Lately, Bruce has been the man of my dreams. Four years ago, he was scrawny but lately, he's been working out. Now he has these bulging muscles that makes my pussy wet every time I look at him. To help deal with his own personal anger, he joined the Bally gym. When I'm down and out and I can't do for myself, that's when Bruce treats me the best. He loves to feel needed. Not to mention, he hasn't struck me one time. Bruce has been waiting on me hand and foot. The only thing I do want to eat is Progresso chicken-noodle soup and saltine crackers. After that, I have my favorite dessert, two sedative pills to help me fall asleep. My body is getting immune to them because I don't get the same effect as before. He has noticed I dropped a few pounds. Once I get my appetite back up, a couple of trips to Fuddruckers for bacon cheeseburgers and Olive Garden's fettuccine Alfredo and my favorite dessert, tiramisu, will get me back to my normal weight. I need some type of professional help because I feel I'm slipping away.

Bruce was really making an effort to cheer me up. Being showered with shopping sprees, jewelry, and a new black BMW didn't even crack a smile on my face. Now, Bruce was taking me away for the weekend. Maybe a change of scenery could get me back to my old self again.

"Where are we going?" I asked while putting on my seat belt.

"You'll see. Before we jump on the highway, I got to make a pit stop," he replied.

"Okay."

* * *

The pit stop was Grandma Elaine's house. It still looked the same. She was waiting for me at the door. My heart started racing. I wasn't ready to deal with her or anything else.

"Izzy, you've been depressed for far too long. I've done everything I could to get you out of this rut you've been in. Yes, you have every right to be pissed off at your father and maybe your mother too, but don't shut your grandmother out of your life. You need to face her as well as your parents. I'll be back on Sunday evening around seven-thirty to pick you up. Open your heart back up, it's never too late to forgive," he explained, rubbing my left cheek and passing me my suitcase.

As soon as I closed the truck door, Bruce was headed toward the stoplight. Slowly, I walked up the front porch stairs. Grandma Elaine was staring me down as I came closer. She opened the door. We embraced each other.

"Grandma, I'm so sorry for ruining your ceremony," I explained.

"Honey, it's all right. I've been missing you, child. You're the only grandbaby I got. Your parents and I didn't realize how angry you were until that day."

"I'm so embarrassed."

"Let it go. Pastor Sears, Pastor Ruff, and the church congregation have no malice in their heart for you."

"Thank you, Grandma Elaine," I responded and smiled.

"Now, that's what I like to see, a smile." *I haven't done it in so long*, I thought.

"Go put your bags up in the spare bedroom. Today, you and I are going in the garden to pick tomatoes, cucumbers, and peaches. We can make a fresh-tossed salad with our baked chicken. Plus, I have a taste for ripe peaches and ice cream."

"I'll be right down," I said, running up the stairs. Then, I realized my family was just what I needed to get myself back together. Still, I wasn't ready to face Mom and my father.

Chapter 25

Vera and her longtime boyfriend, Bernard, tied the knot today, April 15. The event had been in the making for eighteen months. She insisted on the colors of gray and pink. There were nine bridesmaids including myself, Rachel, a maid of honor, a matron of honor, and two junior bridesmaids who wore strapless pink dresses. The groomsmen strutted down the aisle in gray suits with pink vests. In addition, there were four ring bearers and four flower girls who were all dressed in white. The most memorable moment of the wedding ceremony was when the very last flower girl was pulled down the center aisle in a pink decorated wagon by the last ring bearer. Many people were flashing their cameras to capture a mere glimpse of the adorable moment.

Since Bruce got out of bed this morning, he had an attitude with me because I was walking down the aisle with another groomsman who I didn't even know till the wedding. He was one of Bernard's friends. Bruce was in so much of a festive mood that he asked me to marry him. I slowly but surely turned him down in the most subtle voice because I didn't want to hurt his feelings. We weren't ready to get married. I was giving him every excuse I could think of. All Bruce had to show for was two Corvettes, four BMWS, and one 1969 Cadillac. We were still living in an apartment. I suggested a house too many times, but he would tell me a house is too much responsibility. If I could change the hands of time, maybe I should have considered going to college. Now, I'm solely dependent on Bruce. Over the years, I've taken too many beatings. I love him with all my heart but sometimes love just isn't enough to hold a relationship together. The beatings will get worse and marrying him will make it even worse. Not to mention, the man will feel as if he has a tighter hold on me. I'm on my way home but first I need to stop by the drugstore.

I sat, hovered on the toilet, as two blue lines appeared on the pregnancy test. My first thought was not to tell Bruce. On the other hand, he's the father of my child. He has a right to know. I didn't know who to call or what to do. Calling Mom was out of the question. Grandma Elaine wouldn't be too happy. Vera doesn't have time to talk. All she'll be doing for the next two weeks is love-making in Jamaica with her new husband. Rachel was probably knocked out by now. After taking a shower, lotioning my skin, and putting on my pajamas, I went in the living room and plopped myself down on the couch. Fifteen minutes into an old episode of the *Arsenio Hall Show*, I drifted off to sleep.

*   *   *

"Why aren't you in bed?" Bruce whispered, giving me a kiss on the cheek.

"I must have fallen sleep," I yawned and stretched out my body.

"After I put these groceries away, let's go to bed. I'm beat," he replied, shaking his head.

"All right, but first I have something to tell you," I announced, coming into the kitchen.

"What's up?"

"I'm pregnant. I took a test when I got home from the wedding."

"It's not mine."

"What do you mean, it's not yours?" I asked, shocked; in disbelief Bruce is saying this to me.

"Do you want to me to repeat those words? The baby ain't mine. Get it through your head. How do I really know you haven't been with nobody else? Did Theo really rape you or were you asking for it by secretly flirting with him? I killed my best friend over you. Besides, Izzy, you are left here all day and night by yourself. Hmm, I'm quite sure you may get lonely. Izzy, you have plenty of time to go cheat on me. Now, you want to plant another man's baby on me. I'm tired of you living off me, girl," he screamed while plucking my head with his fingers. In this moment, I realized Bruce was only saying all these degrading things to bring me down, break my spirit, so I won't leave him. Yeah, I was dependent on him financially but he definitely became dependent on me to be by his side. Other men were a threat to him and I was getting tired of his jealous ways. This is the end for Bruce and me. Making a promise to myself, I vowed to never accept a man putting their hands on me or degrading me. A real man is supposed to cherish me and lift my spirits up. Even if I wanted to, Bruce would never allow me to get a job. It gives me too much freedom in his eyes.

"And you wonder why I won't marry your sorry ass." Before I knew it, Bruce had me pinned up against the oven. His hands were tightly affixed around my neck so tight I thought I was going to lose consciousness. I grabbed the pan on the stove and hit him as hard as I could in the head. He fell to the floor. I repeatedly kept beating him all over his body with the pan. I even hit him in the dick four times. With each lick I gave him, Bruce sounded more like a wounded dog. Fortunately, my purse was still on the kitchen counter and I managed to pull out the Taser gun. When Bruce appeared to be trying to get up from the floor, I would shock him with the gun over and over again. "This is for every beating, every punch, every kick, and every speck of blood shed of all the times you put your hands on me. You think I'm cheating on you? You've probably been cheating on me all these years. Bruce, you got a guilty conscience."

When I saw him practically going into convulsions, I stopped with the Taser gun in my left hand and the pan in my right. Bruce slowly dragged himself out of the apartment. The day had come to where it would be him or me surviving. I couldn't run because I knew he would find me. I can't live like this anymore. I quickly went into action, putting on my bulletproof vest under my blue sweatshirt and placing the .22-caliber gun in my sweatpants pocket. I called Grandma to let her know I loved her just in case I came out of this apartment in a plastic body bag. Bruce was definitely coming back. Now, all I had to do was wait.

Chapter 26

The clock read seven o'clock in the morning. I haven't moved from the same spot. As soon as the key turned in the door, I got into position behind the door. When Bruce shut it, I splashed a mixture of jalapeño and lemon juice into his eyes. He cried in pain. While covering his eyes, he tried to feel his way to the kitchen. I kept pushing him back. Turning up the stereo, I put in the CD of Kelis's "Caught out There."

"I hate so much right now," I chanted at the top of my lungs over and over again.

As I was about to pull out the gun in my pants pocket, there was a knock at the door. I turned the music down and looked through the peephole. It was a squad team of police.

"Open the door, it's the police," the voice demanded.

"Yes, sir, Officer," I responded after opening the door.

"Ma'am, we have a warrant for the arrest of Bruce Tripson. He's been indicted for six robberies and first-degree murder in the state of Virginia."

"Officers, please come in. I'm so glad you're here. I

was going to call you because Bruce and I got into a fight. He was choking me," I cried out. One of the officers came to my aid to console me. He even was kind enough to give me numbers for help with domestic abuse.

"She did a number on him," the second officer blurted when they picked Bruce up from the floor. He didn't say a word. This day had caught up with him for all of those robberies. The officers didn't seem to care I threw the acidic liquid into his eyes. They were more concerned about getting their man and never bothered to search the apartment.

Chapter 27

Bruce didn't have any money saved in a bank account or had anything stashed away for days like these. All the money in my personal safety box had been spent on clothes and jewelry. Eventually, I stopped putting money in it. I sold all of his cars to friends and associates to round up lawyer money. His lawyer, John Seabram, wanted sixty thousand dollars in cash before Bruce could retain him. With the sale of all his cars, I paid the lawyer and paid up the rent for the apartment for two months just to buy me time. I didn't know what I was going to do. Yeah, I could go live with Grandma Elaine but I didn't want her finding out about the baby. Vera and Bernard didn't need me invading their space. Rachel didn't have room for me in her one-bedroom apartment.

It turns out Bruce's friends of twenty years snitched on him to the police so he could receive a lower sentence. He was indicted on four counts of murder in the first degree and only five counts of armed robbery. The chips were stacking up against him. Bruce wanted to avoid a trial so he took a guilty plea of seventy years to be served at

Greensville Correctional Center in Jarratt, Virginia. To me, he got life. Now I could go on with mine. I never went to see him in jail; however, I did write him to let him know I had an abortion. I didn't want him trying to reach out to our child from behind bars. If he could beat me down, he would do the same to a child. Bruce has written me at least twenty letters telling me how sorry he was for putting his hands on me. To be honest, I don't believe him. Plus, I have the satisfaction of the memory seeing him bent at the knees on the floor with his eyes burning. A part of me wanted to write another letter to him asking how it felt. Someday, I'll find it in my heart to forgive him. In time, I want to have closure on this chapter of my life. What I learned from this experience is that I put a man and his needs before myself and my family. I have wasted eight years of my life with him. Most women would have some of type of skill, trade or a college education. I'm going to have to start from the bottom. The last thing I need is another man. This baby is the only good thing that came out of the relationship with Bruce and me. The choices I make have to be better than this. I'm only twenty-seven years old and have the chance to ultimately change my life around.

Chapter 28

The two months in the apartment passed so quickly. I managed to scrounge up most of my belongings and leave the apartment. The black BMW was damaged due to someone putting sugar in the tank. It would cost thousands to get the engine repaired. Money I didn't have. I was so disgusted with myself for not saving any money. I found refuge in a pregnancy shelter on Princess Anne Road. The center director took me under her wing and I was truly cared for.

I gave birth to a six-pound, eleven-ounce baby girl who I named Sophia. She had my ocean green eyes and curly hair. After careful consideration, I decided to give her up for adoption to a mixed couple who were not able to conceive children. I turned to one of the most reputable adoption agencies in the Hampton Roads area of Virginia. After screening and vigorous background checks, I chose the Weavers to raise my daughter. It was one of the hardest things that I had to do thus far in my life. The Weavers agreed to send me pictures of Sophia. As soon as I was released from the hospital, I set up a post office box. I wanted to see her grow into a young woman. Vera and Rachel are the only ones that know about Sophia and the adoption. Fortunately, the adoptive parents paid all of my medical expenses and gave me five thousand dollars to start a new life.

Chapter 29

Two months later, I'm back living at Grandma Elaine's house. I still have an hourglass figure but I've gone from a size six to a size eight, which I can accept. Not to mention, I could always lose the weight. One of the stipulations of living here is I have to get a job. Grandma Elaine, my friends, and anyone else with their two cents weren't surprised about what happened to Bruce. Vera and Bernard are still enjoying the honeymoon phase. Rachel is pregnant. Not to mention by a married man. I have to admit she did the oldest trick in the book to try to keep him, but she's my friend first. I've been by Rachel's side trying to help her cope with the situation. She is hoping to have a son.

I borrowed Grandma's car to get out of the house. Having a taste for pancakes, turkey sausage, and crisp hash browns, I stopped at the Silver Diner on Virginia Beach Boulevard. Tagging along with me was the wanted ads so I could start looking for employment. Cringing at the thought of getting a job, I circled five listings for administrative-assistant work with my blue pen. Halfway through my meal, I noticed the diner was getting filled up.

"Is anyone sitting here?" a woman's raspy voice asked.

"Well, no, you can sit here too. I'm just about to leave, anyway," I replied. This woman had timeless beauty. She had a frail body frame, pale flawless skin, long black hair, and manicured nails.

"You resemble my daughter, a bit. What's your name?" she asked.

"Izzy—I mean, Isabel Preston. Everyone calls me by my nickname."

"Nice to meet you, Izzy. Do you mind if I smoke around you?"

"Yes, I do. Smoking may kill you. I'm sure your family wants you to be around till you're at least one hundred and fifty."

"You're quite flattering. My name is Opal Claydell. All of my family is in Naples, Italy where I was raised. The rest of my family does come and visit frequently. I did have a daughter but she was killed in a car accident. A drunk driver, who to this day sits behind bars, not remembering what happened that night."

"I'm so sorry for your loss. If you don't mind me asking, how long did he or she get sentenced to?" I asked, picking up on her scent of the perfume, Tuscany.

"Six years."

"Were you in the car when the accident occurred?"

"Yes, it was a wet and rainy night. The truck struck us from behind. If she would have had her seat belt on, she could have lived. I would always tell her to put it on over and over again. She wouldn't, just to be rebellious against me. That's teenagers for you. Enough about me, what's your story? You know, Izzy, I usually don't open up to people but because you resemble . . ."

"What can I get you to drink?" the waitress interrupted.

"A cup of coffee, black. I want to order eggs over easy and wheat toast."

"Will that be all, ma'am?"

"Yes, thank you. Anyway, as I was saying, you resemble my daughter, Carmen."

"Is it because of my green eyes?" I inquired.

"Why, yes it is. How did you know?"

"Lucky guess."

"So what do you do, Izzy?"

"Right now, nothing," I replied, shrugging my shoulders.

"Ah, I see. You don't strike as the nine-to-five type."

"To be honest, I've never had a job before."

"You shouldn't have to work," Opal suggested.

"I see it that way too in a fantasy world. Right now, I'm facing reality and I've got to get a job."

"You can work with me. I will show you how."

"Show me how to do what? What is it that you do exactly?" I asked.

"I'm going to show you how to use what you got to get you what you want. Those green eyes can make a man's heart melt and hefty wallet open. Let me show you the way of mastering the art. Some people call it being a gold digger. I call it men paying to pay for the finer things of life. For example, men will pay good money for a cut of meat cooked to their liking. They will also pay to be entertained and that's simply what I will show you how to do. The rewards are extraordinary. Not to mention, money is no object to these men."

"What's the catch?" I questioned. *Nothing is free in this world.*

"For you, my child, I will charge nothing. You will be

my personal charity case. In memory of my Carmen," she responded.

Opal began to tell me about the upscale escort service she owns in downtown Norfolk in the heart of the Ghent area and what brought her here all of places. She came here from Naples to visit her aunt and uncle thirty years ago and never left. They owned the famous Italian restaurant called Spaghetti. Now, it's closed down because her relatives are deceased. Also, she wanted to flea from her native country because the love of her life died in a fire. Opal tells me the pain from his death scarred her for life. She is incapable of falling in love with another man.

After selling the restaurant, she bought a run-down building and fixed it up. Men who don't make over one hundred thousand dollars a year are not welcome. Opal stated she owned the business so she could make her own rules. I told her my story from start to finish. She sympathized with me about my father and the years of abuse I took from Bruce. Maybe she and I were meant to meet. I was looking for a mother role model and she was craving to fill the void of losing her daughter.

Chapter 30

Opal had a long list of clients who I could pick from. One thing I liked about her place of business is she had tight security. Two huge guards willing to break every bone in your body were in front of the building and in the back.

For three months, Opal had me master the art of gold digging. She was becoming more of a mother figure for me. I respected her because she was so strong and stood up for herself. Not to mention it took a lot of courage to leave her native country of Italy and start a life here. We took frequent trips in the area to scope out new prospects. The local CEOs, club owners, and athletes were easy giveaways.

My wardrobe took a 360-degree turnaround. The various colors of sweat suits in my closet were replaced with expensive dresses and suits. Lingerie was a must. G-strings, thongs, bustiers, and boy shorts were strongly advised. I even brought sexy costumes such as the French maid, wicked witch, nurse, doctor, and the naughty student. In addition, the leather cat costume was the sexiest for me. For men who really paid up to have me in their presence, I purchased several cupless patent corsets. Opal constantly reminded me I was selling a fantasy. Men don't want to see grandma panties. Regularly, I received manicures and pedicures. Keeping up with fashion wasn't difficult at all. She hired a fashion consultant from Los Angeles to explain and show me the importance of appearance and dress. Opal decided against any kind of plastic surgery. She felt women were altering God's creation. Myself, I didn't rule it out. Fortunately, I didn't get any stretch marks from the pregnancy. From the day I found out I was pregnant to the day I had Sophia, I consistently rubbed Palmer's Shea Butter on my breasts, butt, and stomach. To get rid of my pudge, she hired a personal trainer, Frederick, to get me back in shape. The only exercise I have previously done is my arm from the counter to my mouth eating a strawberry sprinkles Dunkin' Donut. Walking from the apartment to the mailbox may count as well. The man earned every penny. At first, I started standing him up because he would want to go running at four in the morning, taking me at least two days to recover. My muscles were so sore I didn't even want to move. Finally, he had grown tired of it and came to my grandmother's house banging on the door. Fortunately, she wasn't there and had gone to the grocery store. One of his hard-core in-your-face pep talks got my behind in gear. Opal liked my long hair but decided it should be long and wavy instead of curly. At Sally's beauty-supply store, I purchased a flatiron. It helped to keep my hair bone straight. Eventually, I would have to move into my own place. Living with Grandma Elaine wouldn't allow me to keep up with this lifestyle.

"Where are you headed off?" Grandma asked while I

was heading out the door and she was folding my laundry.

"I'm going to a small gathering with friends," I explained, feeling bad for lying to her.

"You seem to find another group of friends quickly. You know, Izzy, being a whore and entertaining married men has harsh consequences. I thought you were on the right path? Be careful about the choices you make, for you will pay for them, my darling."

"Grandma, you don't know what you're talking about," I insisted, walking out the door and slamming it behind me.

Tonight, I have a dinner date with one of Opal's long-time clients, Roy Stringer, an oil tycoon from Texas who visits for fun and relaxation. He's staying at the exclusive Regency Hotel, which he owns in Virginia Beach, down by the boardwalk. Stringer isn't much of a social butterfly and prefers to have dinner by candlelight in his room. I knocked on the door, nervous as hell. *What if he didn't like me? What if none of these men like me? I don't have another option. This is my plan A, B, C, and D. I don't want to be at Grandma Elaine's house longer than I have to.*

"Isabel?" he asked.

"Yes, may I come in?" I asked, standing in front of the door. I had on a three-piece red suit as he requested.

"Oh, yes, please come in." Roy Stringer looked to be at least seventy years old. He was more on the plump side.

"Before we get started, let's get down to business. Did you get the ten thousand dollars that I wired to your account?" he inquired.

"Yes, I sure did," I said, nodding. The business portion

is simple. A gentleman can call Opal, her receptionist or myself to set up a meeting. Once the date is confirmed, five to ten thousand dollars would be transferred into my account. Opal charges at least twenty-five hundred as the minimum. To be on the safe side, once the money is transferred, I wire it into another checking account into another bank where no one knows the account number. This was Stringer's usual fee. Opal made all the other ladies pay her a 20 percent fee if it was one of her clients. If a lady tried to cross Opal and not pay the usual fee, she would make her an outcast in the escort world. In turn, no one would want to be bothered with you. If you found a prospect on your own, she agreed to get nothing. She refused to take any money from me, for now. Eventually, I want to start giving her something. If it wasn't for her, I wouldn't be here. I could have been working a nine-to-five job and turned into a certified miserable clock-watcher, hating life.

"Great, let's eat. I'm starving," he stated, rubbing his stomach. We ate on the terrace of his balcony overlooking the beach. It was beautiful. He ordered us roasted duck in a pear glaze, broccoli soufflé, and orzo. Stringer wasn't the dessert type. We talked while we ate.

"Now, time for the fun. I'm going to cut to the chase, honey. I'm too old to screw. My eyes get full enough. At times, I think I'm two heart attacks away from dying. See that machine over in the corner?"

"Yes."

"I want you to get into it, but first slowly take off your clothes. Please, don't be scared of the machine. You'll have a blast, trust me."

"Okay," I agreed, slowly taking off my clothes, revealing a bronze-colored lace teddy. After I was secure into the machine, Stringer turned it on. Suddenly, no one-dollar- but fifty-dollar bills starting seeping through the holes in the machine. It was easier than I thought to catch the money. The air blowing inside was going at a fast pace.

"Grab as many as you can. You got thirty minutes in the machine."

"Can I have five more minutes?" I asked, revealing my right breast and playing with the nipple.

"I'll give you ten," he decided, smiling and sitting back into his chair.

Chapter 31

Three years had passed. Once the money was coming in at a regular pace, I packed my bags at Grandma Elaine's house and moved into a lavish apartment in the sky at the Town Center in Virginia Beach. Years ago, nothing was around here except Pembroke Mall. Now, there's everything you can think of all in one area. The Cheesecake Factory, Max & Erma's, P.F.Chang's, Macaroni Grill, Bravo!, Ruth' Chris steak house, Keegan's, and California Pizza, just to name a few of the restaurants. Various banks are in walking distance. Not to mention various shops such as the Ann Taylor clothing shop, Ficarra Jewelers, Sumatra Salon & Day Spa, and Origins. Everyone was trying to get into the just built Cosmopolitan penthouse apartments. My name had to go on a waiting list. Once approved, I had a two-bedroom apartment that had lots of space. It's just the way I like it. Included were granite countertops, stainless-steel appliances, and custom-made cabinets. The European balcony overlooked most of the Town Center. As an additional bonus, residents were given access to a rooftop pool and cardio-wellness center.

To build up my clientele, I sought the aid of the Internet. I posted a Web site named www.250Kandoverclub.com. Opal's minimum income was bumped to one hundred and fifty thousand dollars. Me, I had to up the stakes. After a couple hours had passed, various men started posted their vital information on the site. It was security protected. To make sure I wasn't wasting my precious time on losers, I had a private investigator who charged me seventy-five dollars an hour, along with a bit of persuasion, to check out each guy. So many leads were coming in that I couldn't seek the attention of every guy, so I cut a deal with some other ladies who did the same profession as me. For every legit lead, I would charge them seven hundred dollars. It was mere pennies compared to what they would be receiving.

Juggling five men isn't easy. Roy Stringer requested to see me three times a month and his fee has moved up to ten thousand each visit. The older men get, the more generous their pockets are. Everyone else is charged five thousand dollars. Money isn't an object to them.

Club owner Miles Walker is squeezed into my schedule twice a month. He has a rock-hard body and a dick so big. After two rounds with him, I have to use K-Y jelly and guzzle down energy drinks to make it through the night. Walker takes forever to cum, which he was, ironically, embarrassed by this. I eased his ego taking in every stroke.

Tall and slim, NBA player Benjamin Anderson is penciled in four times a month. He calls me almost every other day at midnight. I'm clueless about why this particular time, though. Reminding him this is only a business arrangement. Anderson flies me to wherever he is just to get a weekly dose of my pussy.

My next ballplayer, clean cut and short, Nicholas Hammon is married and straight business. It's why we get along so well. Plus, the fact he's impotent. Hammon had considered using Viagra, but I fake it so well he actually thinks I enjoy three-minute sex sessions. No wonder his wife is cheating on him. Less work I have to put out is fine with me.

Curly-haired, blue-eyed CEO Alexander Martin of Avastar, one of the nation's leading cellular phone companies, is gracious enough to give me the latest cell phone technology. He enjoys flying in the sky with his *rented* jet while I suck his dick. Because of the thrill, Martin had my dying to put my lips around it.

The cash is rolling in like clockwork. To show forth all of my good efforts, I have leased a Bentley, Porche, Cadillac Escalade, and a BMW. I own a 2003 burgundy Lexus truck. It's crazy, unbelievable, and exciting to choose which vehicle I want to roll out of the parking garage to drive five days out of the week. The neighbors are guessing about what I do for a living.

Chapter 32

Nothing was planned today until Benjamin text-messaged my cell phone and advised me to meet him at Nordstrom in MacArthur Center Mall by the piano for a well-deserved shopping spree. I began writing down a list of all of the apparel I could rack up from him. Seven and Citizens jeans, new shirts and handbags were at the top of my list. Also, I could stock up on my M•A•C cosmetic products such as Fix-a-Face, which rejuvenates my skin, Lust lip gloss, see-through, floral abundance, and extra powder brushes and mascara.

It was eleven o'clock on a Tuesday morning so a lot of people weren't shifting through the racks. With the hand-written list in my right hand and my Louis Vuitton bag in my left hand, I opened the door. Before going to the piano, I walked to the café for a small cup of coffee. When arriving at the destination, no one was there. It was typical for Ben to be running a few minutes late so I waited. Suddenly I heard a voice behind me.

"Is it Isabel or Diamond?" a woman's voice asked, approaching me.

"Isabel," I said looking her up and down. "Who are you?" I inquired, shrugging my shoulders.

"You know he has another one," she confessed.

"Who is *he*?"

"Benny."

"I don't care. You shouldn't talk to strangers. Haven't you ever heard of stranger danger?" I blurted out and then started walking away, reaching into my handbag for the cell phone to call *Benny*. The bottle of Mace and Taser gun were tucked in my handbag ready to go just in case *she* wanted to put her hands on me.

"I lured you here."

"Why?" *Damn, I'm not going shopping today.*

"I've seen you at some of his games."

"And? What do you want?" I asked, growing tired of her charades.

"To leave him alone."

"Take your concerns up with him. Women like you are pathetic, always wanting to confront the *other* woman." Since she was looking for answers to her burning questions, I was going to give it her and make her ass cry.

"My name is Janell and I'm his fiancée."

"As you already know, my name is Isabel and it's not my fault your Benny would rather be with me than you. Go run along and stop wasting my time."

"Listen to me, I'm pregnant," she commented with tears in her eyes, revealing a pudge that looked around five months.

"I apologize. I'm just at my wit's end," she explained, holding her hands up.

"Dry your damn tears, I don't give a damn about you."

"So what do you want? All gold diggers have a price," Janell stated.

"Now, you're talking sense," I agreed.

"I don't have that much money," she insisted.

"Is that my problem? Now, first, you're going give me a shopping spree courtesy of you and I want thirty-five thousand right now. By the way, I don't take checks, strictly cash and I may consider leaving him alone for thirty-six thousand dollars," I instructed. "Thirty-five is the number of times I screwed him and added one more because I'm about to screw him and his pregnant girl-friend. Not to mention, more money and perks will keep rolling in from him. Is it a deal or not?"

"It's a deal," she agreed and rolled her eyes at me while I handed her an account number to wire the money into.

"Plus, let's head over to the M•A•C counter so you can pick up a few things for me."

The next day, thirty-six thousand dollars was wired into my bank account. Four days later, I was letting Benny eat me in a five-star hotel. This guy could eat pussy and I came every time his tongue played with my clitoris.

Chapter 33

"You wanted to see me, Opal. I got your voice mail," I said, coming into the kitchen. About two years ago, Opal gave me a house key and mailbox key to use when she was on vacation and out of town on business. I would feed her two Siamese twins cats, exotic fish, and water the plants. She lived in Norfolk in the Oceanview area in fairly new-built homes. The housing prices ranged from three hundred and fifty thousand to a million dollars.

"I've made a monster out of you," she remarked, shaking her head while preparing manicotti.

"What are you talking about?" I inquired while getting a spoon from the drawer and stealing ricotta from the bowl while she was hovering over the dishwasher.

"You've mastered the art of playing with men and getting what you want out of them; however, this wasn't intended to be long-term. Three years ago, I met a girl who was in desperate need of help. I figured you would do this for maybe a year or two, and then move on with your life. Now, all you care about is enhancing your looks and

I've seen those magazines you accidentally left at the office about plastic surgery. Plus, I hear everything, Izzy. Men talk just as much as women. You charged a client fifteen thousand for one night with you. Izzy, darling, you're getting greedy."

"He paid it," I spat back, crossing my arms.

"That's not the point."

"Maybe I've been going a little overboard, so what. This is all I have right now. I'm going to enjoy every minute of it," I replied, taking a seat at the kitchen bar.

"Promise me you'll consider getting out of this lifestyle. Sleeping with a lot of different men for a long period of time isn't good for the soul or your vagina. Each and every person has a one true love. Once you find that person, cherish him, hold on tight, and never let go of that man. Taking someone for granted is far worse than a slap in the face. Also, I want you to think about mending the relationship with your mother."

"Okay, I'll consider quitting the lifestyle. As far as my mother is concerned, I'm still not ready. It's still hurts," I said, giving her a hug and rolling my eyes when she couldn't see. "Since you're asking for a favor, I want one as well."

"Name it," she insisted with her hands on her hips.

"I want you to quit smoking."

"All right, I was planning to go on the patch on Sunday."

"Great," I announced.

"One more thing," she requested. "Start saving your money. Retirement should be a priority. Your looks won't get you by forever. To prove it to you, this is me at your age. Now, look at me now," she insisted, holding a picture of herself.

"Opal, you're gorgeous, then and now."

"On this subject, flattery will get you nowhere, but

thank you. Izzy, you have nothing but leased cars to show for your efforts. If you break away from this life, I will pay half for a house for you. Enough talk about business, start making the Greek salad," she instructed, getting the olives out of the refrigerator.

Opal has always treated with me like I was her daughter. Since I haven't talked to my mother in years, it was good to have her around. She was always honest with me; she had to be for the type of business we were in, but it was more than that. She would never lie to me because she knows I'm strong enough to handle the truth. I loved that about her and would do anything she asked of me, including possibly giving up the business.

We ended our conversation over a quiet dinner of chicken marsala and Greek salad and a nice Riesling wine while enjoying the view of the skyline from her penthouse apartment.

Chapter 34

After ejaculating in a condom, Miles Walker laid on top of me and fell asleep. Now he made my skin crawl. Walker had become comfortable with me and let himself go, literally. Tonight, we went to Salsa, a Mexican restaurant on Indian River Road in Virginia Beach. The man is forty-six years old. He should know refried beans don't mix well with his digestive system. While on top, he farted more times than he penetrated my pussy. I pondered how I got to this point in my life, wondering even more when and how can I get out of this lifestyle.

The following week, Bill Winslow, owner of a multi-billion-dollar paper company, was the best piece of meat I've ever had. Out of all the men I dealt with, he could make me cum. In our first sexual encounter, he had me buck naked, harnessed in a swing, holding on tightly to the handlebars as he fucked me. The next was even better. Facedown on the edge of the bed, he picked me up by my legs and his dick gladly found its way into my pussy. Following that was when I got up on top of a mechanical bull-riding machine while Winslow watched. Shifting back and forth and still trying to keep my balance drove me wild. After getting off of the machine, I climbed on top of him and came after five minutes. After I noticed a disappointed look on his face, I had to give him another go-round for coming so fast. Winslow didn't prefer using condoms; he had no choice with me. He may want to live on the wild side; me, on the other hand—the AIDS special on BET petrified me. If there's anything I can do to prevent it, it will get done. I love myself too much to die like that. In this business, I have no choice but to be extra careful. Refusing to become a statistic, I bring my own Magnum condoms.

Winslow and I had come from the Scorpio, an open bar, lounge, and restaurant in downtown Norfolk. After sipping on two bottles of 1947 cheval blanc wine, which can cost more than fifteen-hundred dollars per bottle, he and I were very drunk and also very horny. Driving drunk wasn't my thing but I never let any of my men pick me up. I always drove just in case there was an emergency and I had to leave.

Once we arrived at his mansion in Suffolk, I ran quickly to the bedroom door, hinting to him I was eagerly anticipating our next sex go-round. The orgasms he had me experience were becoming more addicting almost to the point where I needed to pay him for his services.

"Take off your dress, slowly," he instructed, stopping at his bedroom door.

"Anything else you want me to take off?" I inquired.

"Don't take off those red pumps," he insisted, looking down at them and coming toward me.

He backed me into the dresser drawer. Next, after I got on four legs, he ripped my grape-colored G-string off. Winslow hungrily started eating my pussy. Back and forth, his tongue stroked my clitoris in a rhythmic motion.

"Say my name when you cum," he begged. I was getting lost in a trance.

"Winslow," I barely said when I did cum.

"Now for the surprise," he blurted out, almost out of breath.

Another woman wearing a see-through corset walked into the room. She tongue-kissed Winslow and then tried to kiss me. I quickly pulled away.

"What's wrong, Izzy? I thought you would like her. Anna is beautiful, isn't she? Now, I know you can't possibly be jealous, there's plenty of Big Daddy to go around," Winslow explained, grabbing his dick.

"Winslow, I love pleasing you, but there are just some things I won't ever do and that's a threesome."

"First time for everything, baby," he insisted, holding up his hands.

"You must be hearing what you want. I don't get down like that," I explained for the last time, searching for my dress and purse off of the beige carpet floor.

"I've give you six thousand more. Come on, Izzy, you're ruining the moment. I've got to bust into something. Otherwise, I'll get a bad case of blue balls."

"You have Anna to bust in. Thanks, but no thanks." I've got to take a stand on something.

"Izzy, don't leave."

"Enjoy the rest of your night. By the way, I'm not jealous," I responded and blew him a kiss while I walked out the bedroom, heading downstairs and walking out of the house. Grateful, I let a deep sigh of relief in the car, very thankful I had driven my Escalade. *I already got my usual fee and came during oral sex. What more can I ask for?* I thought, putting on my seat belt and backing out of the driveway.

Chapter 35

"Hello?" I answered the cell phone.

"Izzy, I've been calling you for weeks now," Winslow ranted in an irritated tone.

"I've been busy. Besides, you crossed the line. You could have at least asked me before bringing Anna into the picture."

"Ah, I see. I didn't realize women like you have standards," he giggled in a devilish tone.

"Do me a favor."

"You should be doing me a favor after that stunt you pulled on me," he responded.

"Go to your doctor and get some dick-enhancing drugs. News flash, the only thing big about you is your credit card limit. When I was with you, I faked it every time. Lose my number, Winslow."

"Izzy," he screamed. Before he realized it, I hung up on him. After hanging up the phone, I laughed to myself. I lied about him having a small dick. I only said it to hurt his feelings. He was a jerk. Winslow should have had the decency to ask first if I wanted to take part in a threesome. Now, I have to start screening my calls and slowly weaning myself away from these men. I had to admit I was going to miss Miles, Benny, Nicholas, and Alexander. More importantly, I was going to truly miss their money being transferred to my checking account.

I'm on way to Grandma Elaine's house to take her to the doctor at Depaul Medical Center. Within the past two months of me visiting her out the house, she has fainted a couple of times. I begged her to let me take her to the hospital, but she always refused. Today, I'm not taking *no* for an answer. Plus, Grandma has been complaining of being thirsty all the time, fatigue and her feet aching. I even took her to a massage therapist so she could get some relief. These days, it's hard for her to get around. There's nothing I wouldn't do for her. Still, I don't let her tell me anything about Mom or my father. To make it through the years, I prefer not to talk about them.

"Thank you for taking me to the doctor. As old I am, I may not pass the driver's test to renew my license because my eyes are getting so bad. Last, the eye doctor told me I have a bit of cataracts in both of my eyes," she explained, getting into the car.

"Between Mom and me, we'll do whatever it takes. Even if you have to come live with me, Grandma, so be it."

"Honey, you're sweet, but the last thing you need is an old lady coming to live with you. The good Lord may call me any day now at the rate I'm feeling."

"Grandmas are supposed to live forever, taking care of their grandchildren and making endless sugar and chocolate chip cookies," I complained. I couldn't stand it when she talked like that. Losing her would be losing half of my heart.

"Ms. Sinclair, please come on back," the nurse assistant greeted us in the waiting room. This office was fast and efficient. We only had to wait ten minutes.

"I'm going to with you," I insisted, holding Grandma's hand. After an extensive questionnaire and the testing of her blood and urine, the doctor walked in.

"Hi, Ms. Sinclair, I'm Dr. Tucker," he greeted her and me while looking down at her medical chart. After thoroughly washing his hands, he checked her breathing and each quadrant of her stomach.

"So, what's going on, Doc?" I eagerly asked in anticipation.

"And you are?" he asked, extending his left hand.

"Izzy, I mean Isabel Preston. I'm her granddaughter," I replied, shaking his head.

"You certainly are beautiful. Are those your real eyes?" he inquired.

"Did you pass the MCAT?" I spat back at him in irritation. Grandma sat in the chair giggling.

"I apologize, Ms. Preston. I hope you don't think I was trying to make a pass at you."

"No, I didn't, because if you were, it would have been a weak one. A doctor of your caliber and prestige trying to get with a concerned patient's granddaughter isn't a good idea. I happened to notice all your credentials from the Virginia Commonwealth University of Medicine. Plus, I see a shiny gold ring on your third finger on your left hand. Now, getting back to the matter at hand, what's wrong or going on with my grandmother, Elaine Sinclair?"

"Oh, yes, Ms. Sinclair, you have diabetes," he managed to say, breaking into a sweat. Years ago, Opal also taught me the art of being nice, but nasty. She consistently reminded me I don't need to curse to get my point across to someone.

"Is it type one or two?" I asked. Last night, I was looking up the symptoms of diabetes.

"It's type two."

"What does this mean for me?" Grandma asked with her hands up.

"Well, I'm not going to put you on medication, yet. First, I want to see if we can get this under control by changing your diet and exercise. To be honest, if you were willing to lose around ten or fifteen pounds, it would help. The foods you are accustomed eating that high in fat and sugar must be eaten in moderation. You want to consume less sugar, Ms. Sinclair. I'm going to set you up with a nutritionist who specializes in diabetes. On your way out, the nurse will give some pamphlets on healthy eating habits and portion control. In addition, I have ordered a machine for you to check your blood twice a day, once in the morning and once in the evening. I would like for you to record your results. This way, you and I can keep track of the results. Are there anymore questions you may have for me, Ms. Sinclair or Ms. Preston?" he asked, looking like a defeated puppy dog.

"No," Grandma responded, letting out a sigh of relief.

"I want to see you back in three months," he stated, shook Grandma Elaine's hand, and walked out of the room.

"Where do you want to go for lunch, Grandma?" I asked, pulling out of the parking lot.

"Picadilly's," she replied.

"I'm glad we figured out what's going on with you. So why the long face for?"

"Child, I don't know if I can or even want to change my eating habits. I've been eating like this all my life."

"Grandma, you and I both know it will not be easy, but Mom and I will help you. She will definitely look at this as a challenge to master."

"Thanks, baby. You always know how to make Grandma feel good."

"You're welcome. So instead of your usual fried fish, mashed potatoes, and sweet potatoes, why don't we both try baked fish, steamed vegetables, and sweet potatoes. For dessert, we could get fresh fruit. Let's drink glasses of water instead of sweet tea."

"Well, I'm willing to try it."

After dropping Grandma off at her house, I drove by Mom's house, parking the car across the street. I sat there just staring at the house. My father had come out to pick up the mail. Shortly after, Mom pulled into the driveway. I slid down in my seat even further. While eating my leftover watermelon and cantaloupe from Picadilly's, I wondered whether or not I should go talk to her.

The clock read ten-thirty PM. I must fallen asleep watching the *Bernie Mac Show* on UPN. The doorbell was ringing. I grabbed the robe in the closet and dashed to the door. Looking through the peephole, it was Vera.

"Izzy, I don't know what I'm going to do," she proclaimed and barged into the door. Vera was drunk.

"What's going on?" I asked while tying my robe together.

"Bernard still isn't out of law school. He doesn't graduate till next May. All the household income is solely dependent on me. Well, today upper management all received pink slips. We're the first to go. The company is downsizing. I went home earlier and Bernard is going to quit law school and get a job to make ends meet. Lord knows where I'm going to find a job with the market being so rocky. No jobs are secure anymore. Besides, Izzy, I don't want him quitting law school. He's worked so hard to stay in. What am I going to do? What if the house gets foreclosed on? You know, Bernard and I are too proud to go to our parents," she said, bursting into tears.

"I'll give you five thousand dollars," I replied, reaching in my purse for the checkbook and proceeding to write out the check.

"Izzy, you know I can't do that," she said, shaking her head and refusing to take the check as I was attempting to place it in her hand.

"Girl, yes you can. Vera, pay up your bills for as long as you can. That way, you won't be so stressed about finding a job. Things happen. This is not a situation where Bernard and you are financially irresponsible. You're trying to put your husband through school and maintain a household. If you need more, let me know. Look at this as a blessing—when one door closes, another one will open."

"Izzy, thank you so much," she announced and finally took the check.

"You're welcome. Vera, you are family to me. I don't know what I'd do without you. Now, I'll fix you some food so you can sober up from all that alcohol you drank. I can smell apple martinis on your breath."

"I'll make some eggs and toast. You can make the turkey sausage links," she said while smiling.

"All right," I agreed.

Chapter 36

Getting rid of Miles Walker wasn't easy. He was relentless on getting me back. Finally after four months, he got the picture. Benjamin Anderson admitted to me that he already had someone else on the side and now had a wife. I simply congratulated him with a hug and sent him on his way. Nicholas Hammon understood I was getting out of the business and I referred him to one of my business associates. Last but not least on the list was Alexander Martin. Somehow, I was going to break the news to him that I was getting out of the business for good. Breaking the news to him wouldn't be easy. We were at Norfolk International Airport at five in the morning to catch a seven AM flight to reach the island of Fiji. Just my luck, I was randomly selected to have my bags checked.

"Are you going to have gloves while checking my things?" I asked in irritation, wearing a light yellow baby-doll dress.

"Ma'am, this won't take long," the airport employee assured me. Meanwhile, Alexander was in the back of the building talking on his cell phone talking business, I suppose.

The check was going smoothly. I knew all rules and regulations of what you could and could not carry on a plane. Since 9/11, airports have gotten strict. Before I knew it, the female employee found my brown chocolate dildo in the plastic Ziploc bag. She accidentally turned it on and didn't know how to turn it off. Other people were starting to stare. Breaking out in sweat, I could hear snickers coming from people all over. Needless to say, I was embarrassed and so was she. Thank goodness I had on sunglasses.

"Are you almost done here?" Alexander asked her, looking down at his watch as he came up from behind me. Luckily, I turned it off and she placed it back into the suitcase where it belonged before he could get an eyeful.

"If sales keep increasing, I'm looking into investing in my own jet," he said while sitting back in our first-class seats.

"You deserve it for all the hard work you put in. Pulling fifteen hours day, six days a week isn't easy."

"I'm glad someone appreciates a hardworking man," he replied and gave me a small peck on the lips. Alexander decided to watch the movie, *Man on Fire* with Denzel Washington while I slept through most of the flight.

Arriving in Fiji, we were greeted by the locals. The people were nice and hospitable, opening their island to us. It was so beautiful and peaceful. I couldn't wait to lie on the white sandy beaches and jump in the crystal blue water; but Alexander and I were starving. We decided to go to a restaurant called Singh's Curry House. There, we

enjoyed overlooking the view of the mountains and ordered two spicy chicken dishes packed full of flavor, rice,
and steamed vegetables.

As the days followed, we enjoyed the three rounds of
sex, hiking—I brought along trail mix to keep my energy
up—bicycling, and horseback riding along the moun-
tainous area of Nadi. Staying at a resort along the Coral
Coast, a butler was available to us twenty-four hours a
day. I was getting used to eating blueberry pancakes, turkey
bacon, and fresh fruit every morning in bed. Today, we
spent the day doing underwater snorkeling. Plus, we
headed to the Astrolabe Reef, near Kadavu, so Alexander
could participate in a friendly surfing competition. He
told me for the rest of the day, I looked the sexiest out of
all the women in my peach bikini, rooting him on to win.

Tired and beat-up from the waves, Alexander wanted
to enjoy an evening in our twenty-five-hundred-square
foot hotel room complete with a sauna, Jacuzzi, and a
private pool. He even let me have an extra hour for the
masseuse to massage my skin. This was the life and I
surely was going to miss it.

"Isabel, I have to something to tell you," Alexander
stated as we enjoyed jumbo tiger prawns and steamed
lobster by candlelight. I knew whatever he had to say
was serious because he never called me by real name unless it was an important matter.

"Alexander, I'm listening, baby," I assured him while
sipping on a glass of Chardonnay white wine.

"I'm getting older now, and facing forty. I'm honored
to have met you, Isabel. You're kind, sexy, sweet, and always know how to put a smile on my face. I'm in love

with you. You never nag me and understand that I will forever be a workaholic. The times that I do want to get away and take time off, I wouldn't be with anyone else besides you. What this boils down to is you getting out of the escort business and becoming my wife," he explained, getting down on one knee with a four-karat princess diamond ring with one karat on each side of the ring. Speechless, I started crying. I knew my men might have cared about me but not enough to make me a wife.

"Alexander, I have something to tell you too."

"The only thing I hope to hear is that you will say yes."

"Well, I'm getting out of the business and hope to venture out on my own. I don't have a plan yet, but I'm resilient and will find something to sink my hands into."

"Please say yes. We're meant to be together. It's not a coincidence that I want to make you mine and you want to get out of the business at the same time."

"I can't accept your proposal. I'm still growing as a woman and a person, trying to find my way through life. I hope you can understand that." Besides, I wasn't in love with him. It's the only way a man can get me down the aisle of matrimony.

"In fact, I'm disappointed. Hopefully, you'll have me as your friend who will always be there for you. In case you change your mind, let me know," he explained, holding up his wineglass.

"All right, thank you so much for being understanding."

"To friendship and happiness," he announced as we toasted.

"Here's your ring back," I said, sliding it to his side of the table.

"You can have it as a token of our friendship."

"Are you sure?" I asked with hesitation.

"I'm sure, besides, my pride won't let me return it to

the jewelry store." We both laughed as I put the ring on the middle finger on my right hand.

Upon arriving home from the best relaxation I've ever had, I was confident that I had made the right decision. Hopefully, I'll find my way in this crazy world we call life. Paying two thousand a month in rent was becoming a waste to me. Now I was ready to start looking for a house to own.

Chapter 37

It was a twenty-minute wait at Mabel's soul food restaurant. My taste buds were craving fried catfish, sweet potatoes with lots of cinnamon and sugar, and okra.

"Number twenty-three, your order is ready," the cashier announced, bagging it together. Looking down at my slip, I noticed my number was thirty-one.

"Izzy," a voice called out.

"Hey, Alicia, how have you been, girl?" I asked, giving her a hug. Her using me for money, I let it go years ago. For all the time that had passed, I felt guilty for not speaking up to Alicia, begging her to get help back then. I had to admit giving her money helped ease my guilt somewhat. Hoping she was drug-free, I managed to work up the nerve to ask her. "So . . . ?"

"Am I clean?" she asked, cutting me off.

"Yeah, I do want to know," I responded.

"I've been clean for a year now. Lord knows, it hasn't been easy."

"How are your parents doing?"

"They're fine, as far as I know. They gave up on me years ago. To tell you the truth, I can't blame them," she explained, shrugging her shoulders.

"I'm proud of your progress."

"Izzy, I take it day by day.

"How's Rachel and Vera doing?"

"Rachel is doing all right. Her son, Michael, is four now. Can you believe it?"

"Last time I saw him, he was barely a month."

"Time sure does fly."

"Isn't that the truth," she giggled.

"Vera is in between jobs right now. Her husband recently graduated Regent University with a law degree. He wants to go into entertainment law," I stated.

"That is so wonderful. How about you? Have you patched things up with your parents yet?"

"I'm fine, thinking seriously about making a career change. Mom and my father are fine, I guess."

"Have the *three of you* patched things up?" she asked, rephrasing the question.

"The only patching up I will do is with Mom. No, we haven't as of yet. To be honest, I don't know if we ever will. Where are you staying at?" I asked, quickly changing the subject. Whenever anyone asks me about Mom or my father, my hearts starts to race. Why, I don't know. It could be anxiety.

"I'm staying at the Salvation Army women's shelter on Colley Avenue in Norfolk. I have two more weeks to stay there till my apartment is ready to move in. I'm so excited. It's a one-bedroom apartment off of Ingleside Road."

"Congratulations."

"Thank you so much. Striving to get my life on track is a constant struggle within myself. I don't have a lot of support these days. Being hooked on heroin and cocaine for over thirteen years, people start giving up on you. My father will not even look at me. Six years ago, I stood at the doorstep of the house I grew up in. He told that he no longer had a daughter and slammed the door in my face. Until I made the personal decision to get help, there wasn't anything anyone could do for me but feed my habit. I know I have used you and other people close to me to get drugs. I want to let you know that I apologize for using your kindness for weakness," Alicia explained in tears. She looked better than the last time I saw her. Crack had aged Alicia, beyond her years. Rachel, Vera, Alicia, and I were all pushing our mid-thirties; however, Alicia appeared to look forty-five. Plus, she had lost a few of her teeth.

"I accept your apology with open arms. I'll tell you what, as a gift for you starting over your life, Alicia, I will arrange for you to stay at the Radisson in downtown Norfolk for two weeks. Check in around three this afternoon. Here's my cell phone number to let me know you got settled in and just in case you need anything else," I explained while jotting it down on my slip.

"Number thirty-one, your order is ready," the cashier announced.

"Thank you so much," she said hugging me again and giving me her cell phone number.

"No problem, that's my order she's calling. I'll talk to you later," I stated with a huge grin in my face, hoping this time Alicia would truly get herself together.

Chapter 38

"Where are we going tonight?" I asked, buckling my seat belt in Vera's Ford Explorer.

"I'm taking you to Ruth's Chris to celebrate. Rachel is meeting us there," she stated.

"What's the occasion?" I asked.

"Your're looking at the new president of the claims department for the Hampton Roads Area of Healthtime insurance company."

"Congratulations," I screamed.

"I received a twenty percent raise from my old salary plus an excellent benefits package. Girl, they match one dollar and twenty-five cents to every dollar I put into my four-oh-one-k plan. Plus, Bernard and I can pay you sooner than I hoped."

"What money? I have no idea what you're talking about. Didn't I tell you that things were going to work out? Now Vera, look back and remember you made it through."

"Yeah, you're right. Bernard is at home studying for the bar," she replied, taking a deep breath.

"After dinner, I got tickets for us to see the comedian Small Fire at the Funny Bone comedy club."

"How's Ms. Little Sophia doing?"

"Getting big of course," I replied while rummaging through my purse for my little photo album.

"Izzy, the girl is a spitting image of you," Vera suggested.

"Laura, her mother, still sends me pictures of Sophia every six months."

"What are her grades looking like?"

"She got accepted to the gifted program at school. I'm excited about that. Currently, she's gearing up for soccer and takes art classes on Saturdays. The girl is talented. Now, if Sophia could just grown out of eczema, she will be fine. The itching gets so bad Laura or John have to give her an antihistamine to stop her from itching almost every night."

"Hopefully, she'll grow out of it," Vera stated, concerned; driving up in the parking garage. Friday nights at the town center mean large crowds. She ended up parking on the fourth floor.

Halfway through the meal, Rachel showed up.

"Sorry I'm late. My sister Kelly took her sweet time getting to the apartment. I'm in need of a drink."

"How does the meal taste?" the waiter asked, eager to fulfill our every need. I could tell he was attracted to my green eyes and 38D breast size. The V-neck black shirt accented them very well. Plus, he gave Rachel a menu to look over.

"May I please have an apple martini?" Rachel asked, finally grabbing his attention.

"Sure. Does anyone need anything else?"

"Yes, I'll have the rum raisin bread pudding," I replied. The medium-well porterhouse steak, full loaded baked potato, and fresh steamed vegetables were good, but the bread pudding is the true reason why I keep coming back to this restaurant.

"Miss, would you like to place an order?" the waiter asked Rachel.

"No, I can't afford these high prices," she insisted, skimming through the menu.

"Very well," he responded and took her menu.

"Congrats on the new job," Rachel announced to Vera.

"Thank you," she replied before sipping on her watermelon martini.

"So, what's going on with you, Izzy?" Rachel inquired.

"I've been taking some business classes at Tidewater Community College. I'm not sure what I want to do yet, though. What I do know is that I do pretty good with numbers. I made the right move by getting out of the escort service."

"You certainly did. On judgement day or probably way sooner than that, God is going to punish you for messing with married and taken men. Izzy, you made a career out of this," Rachel said, shaking her head.

"I don't know what God you serve, but my God doesn't punish people. As far as Michael, I did what I could. Besides, if you want to get technical, Michael is your son who you spread your legs open to conceive and makes him your responsibility. You're one to talk."

"What are you trying to say?"

"I'm not trying to say anything, because I was going to say it before you gently cut me off. Since you want to air dirty laundry, let's bring out your smelly-ass closet. You get pregnant on purpose by a fifty-five-year-old *married* man who told you before he didn't want to have any more kids. Damn, you *tried* the oldest trick in the book and it backfired on you. Not only did he divorce his first wife but married another woman. Being a good friend, I never judged you. Instead, I was there for you and my godson, Michael."

"Whatever," she stated and rolled her eyes.

"Yeah, same to you before you open your mouth, think about what comes out. Before and while Michael's father was with you, he used my old escort service. I tried to warn you, but you thought I was so-called jealous. Now, with his new wife whom he must love, I haven't seen him in the office or his credit cards on the monthly invoices in a while. Actually, it's been about eighteen months since he used those services. Hmm, wasn't that around the same time that he got married to his second wife at the botanical gardens? Isn't that the most luxurious flower haven where you wanted to marry him at?

"That's enough," Rachel demanded.

"You started it and if you would shut the hell up, I can finish. Don't get mad at me because you hate your job and your life spending all your money hiring a private investigator to watch the man's every move. Rachel, you know he's married and moved on with his life so stop watching his every move and start watching your credit card. Private investigators are not cheap. To mention money, who was there for you when you almost got evicted? Who cleared your checking when you had a twenty-five-hundred-dollar garnishment from the Internal Revenue Service? Or when you couldn't pay Michael's day care, who came through for you?" I questioned.

"You did," she murmured.

"Ah, I see. Now that you go to church six nights a week and managed to get married in the name of the Lord, now you of all people want to get holy and sanctified. Don't bite the hand that has helped you over and over and over again. I've dealt with your countless excuses, immaturity, and irresponsibility."

"I'm leaving, I don't have to take this. Besides, Vera, you're not even sticking up for me," Rachel spat back and stood up with her purse in her hand.

"You started this fight. I'm out of it, Rachel. You're not going to ruin my night with your negativity. We all know at this table what you have done, I've done, and Izzy has done. For you to sit here and say God's going to punish her, that's wrong, dead wrong," Vera insisted, looking right into Rachel eyes.

"Good night," Rachel stated with tears in her eyes as she was heading toward the exit of the restaurant.

"Rachel," I called out.

"What do you want?"

"Oh nothing, I want you to realize, Jeff, your new husband, currently uses the escort service as well. I still help Opal with the bookkeeping part of the business. Where is he tonight? Hmm, another late night at the trucking company? Maybe if you didn't nag a man so bad, maybe they would stick around for longer than six months. Give Michael my best," I stated with a spiteful tone and waved good-bye to her with a smile.

Later on that night, on the comedy club, Vera and I laughed so hard our stomachs were hurting.

Chapter 39

"Hello," I answered my cell phone.

"Hi, may I speak with Isabel Preston, please?"

"This is she, may I ask who's calling?"

"Of course, my name is Elliot Cannon, the general manager at the Radisson Hotel."

"Yes, sir."

"We have a problem with the room you charged for a Ms. Alicia Stinman."

"What's the problem?" I asked. "I talked to her the other day and she told that she checked out after the two weeks had expired."

"Yeah, she checked out all right, but took everything out of the room. I mean, everything, literally."

"What do you mean?"

"The room is bare. Everything is gone except the sink, tub, the drawers, and the bed."

"How did she get everything out with no one seeing her? More importantly, how can I fix this?" I asked, shrugging my shoulders.

"We think she had some assistance, but most likely it was done late at night. She must have used the back door. Only the television and the computer were stolen from the room. I talked to my district manager. If you could come up with seven hundred and fifty dollars, this matter will be resolved.

"I'll be on my way around noon. In return, I would like a letter stating that the damages have been paid in full and I will face no further action taken by the hotel."

"The letter will be done by the time you get here. Thank you for choosing the Radisson Hotel and for your promptness in this matter," he stated.

"You're welcome."

As soon as I hung up the phone, I dialed Alicia's cell phone number only for it to be a disconnected number. I could have called the Salvation Army women's shelter to see if they had a forwarding address but I didn't have the energy. I had an accounting test to get to in an hour. Besides, karma will creep up on Alicia sooner or later.

Relieved the test was over, I could continue on with my day. As I was leaving the hotel with seven hundred and fifty dollars less than what I had before, I walked out with the letter in hand as a man tapped me on the shoulder.

"Yes, how can I help you?" I asked, turning around and looking up and down at the six-foot middle-aged man.

"Excuse, miss, sorry to bother you, but are you related a woman named Opal Claydell? You resemble her daughter," he asked eagerly.

"Who wants to know?" I inquired.

"My name is Jimmy Risoto. I'm an old friend of hers

from Naples, Italy," he stated. My heart started racing. He is Opal's long lost true love. Every chance the woman gets, she tells me stories of their romance love affair.

"Stay right here, Mr. Risoto. I'll be right back. I need to use the restroom," I responded while rummaging through my purse for the cell phone. Once inside the bathroom, I dialed Opal's number.

"This is Opal," she answered.

"He's here," I proclaimed.

"Who's he, darling?" she asked.

"Jimmy Risoto, he's here at the Radisson Hotel. To make a long story short, I paid for my ex-friend Alicia to stay here for two weeks. Well, she stole a few items out of the room. Pissed off, I came up here to pay for the damages and I ran into him. He said that I resembled your daughter," I explained.

"Listen to me carefully, Izzy, did you happen to notice a brown birthmark on his neck?" she asked with pure excitement in her voice.

"Yes, ma'am. It was on the left side of his neck in the middle."

"Oh my, it is him. Bring him to the house in fifteen minutes. I've got to get dressed."

"Wear something sexy," I blurted out.

"I'm looking in my closet now," she answered and hung up the phone. Remaining calm, I told Mr. Risoto to follow me in his vehicle.

"How is she doing? Where does she live? Are you her daughter?" he inquired, dying to know each answer.

"She's fine; living in the city of Norfolk. Her house is huge. You will see, sir. No, I'm not her daughter. She died in a car accident years ago, long before I met Opal," I explained.

"Oh, I see. I'm the father of her daughter. I would have

loved to see my only daughter," he stated with disappointment.

"I'm sure Opal can explain more about the incident. Make sure to keep up with me. I drive fast, Mr. Risoto. We're not too far away from Opal's house."

The drive to her house took longer than I thought. There was a six-car pileup going on to Interstate 64 West. A usual fifteen-minute drive took thirty minutes. Mr. Risoto and myself, along with the other drivers, inched our way through the traffic.

"Are you ready to come in?" I asked, turning the key.

"You better believe it. I've spent many years searching high and low for this woman," he explained. Opal never told me what truly happened. Why did she leave Naples? Why didn't Mr. Risoto know about his daughter dying?

After I opened the door, Opal greeted Mr. Risoto in the foyer. For at least ten minutes, those two lovebirds gazed into each other's eyes.

"How did you find me?" she asked while coming close to him with tears in her eyes.

"A costly private investigator. Why did you leave me?" he inquired.

"Papa's men would have killed you if we would have stayed together, so I came here to Virginia after my Aunt Audrey and Uncle Vincent moved here. Papa and Ma loved Carmen, our daughter, as if she was their own. To be honest, she was one spoiled young lady. Even though Papa demanded, I never gave him the name of the father of Carmen."

"Back then, I was a big boy. You could have at least told me the truth. I could have come here to see you and Carmen. Now, I'll never get to meet her. I know she was gorgeous just like her mother," Jimmy explained with tears in his eyes.

"I have plenty of home movies. Last year, I put them all on one DVD. Deep down, I knew someday you would find me."

"Opal, after more than thirty years since we met, I'm still in love with you. There's not a day that went by that I didn't think about what could have been. Sure, I've had flings here and there but nothing concrete."

"I'm so sorry that I hurt you. Now, Ma and Pop are in their eighties. Our families not getting along shouldn't even matter anymore."

"Umm, before I vomit because I know you two are going to kiss any minute now, I'm going to leave. Opal, I'll call you in a couple of days," I explained, heading toward the door.

"You're not going anywhere, Izzy. Please stay and share in this joyous occasion. This is just a firm confirmation that I was meant to meet you. Honestly, you could have told Jimmy, no, I don't know who Opal is but you didn't. Instead, you brought him right to me. I'm truly grateful to you for the rest of my life," she explained, hugging me.

"Opal, I'm still going to leave. Seriously, Mr. Risoto and you need some time to talk and get reacquainted with each other," I whispered in her ear.

"Nonsense, besides, I made reservations at Alexander's on the Bay for the three of us."

At the restaurant, Jimmy and Opal talked about growing up in Naples. I hoped to one day find my one true love. Hoping is one thing but finding him is another. Looking back, I can only say that I was in love with Bruce, the one side of him that was sweet, encouraging, and a good man. Soon, love tarnished into pure hate. At times, I think about if the police hadn't barged into the apartment, I would have killed him with one gunshot to the head for everything he put me through. Sitting here with these lovebirds made me think of my parents. Plus, I longed for a man to love me with all his heart and grow old with that person. Most of all, because Opal chose to flee her native country for fear Jimmy's life would be in danger, it took thirty years for the two to be reunited. It goes back to what Mom said: life will consists of many choices.

During dinner, I noticed Opal looked mighty pale. Her usual glow of beauty was fading away. She's probably stressed about the Internal Revenue Service auditing her books for last year. Later on that night, Opal showed Jimmy and me countless pictures of Carmen and herself over the years. When she put in the DVD of all the home videos she had made, I took it as my cue to leave.

It was time for Jimmy and her to have some time, alone. On the way home, I began thinking even more about Mom. I don't want thirty years to go by before I speak to her again.

Chapter 40

Fall semester at Tidewater Community College was a success. I received two As and two Bs. In the spring, I plan to take some online business courses. I prefer not to be confined to a classroom. I'm attending college because it interests me to learn new things. Besides, one day I wouldn't mind running my own business. As an early Christmas present for myself, I brought a Dell laptop computer.

Spending the Christmas holiday with Vera and Grandma Elaine was so much fun. Vera and I decorated the tree on Christmas eve. We stayed up all night talking about old times while sipping on hot chocolate spiked with rum. The next day, Grandma made a feast including turkey, stuffing, macaroni and cheese, fresh-made rolls, cranberry sauce, and sweet country ham all for me with all the other Christmas trimmings. I came over later after Mom and my father dropped by.

"Izzy, how long are you going to keep avoiding your mother?" Grandma asked while we sat in the living room.

"I'm so glad you're doing much better with the diabetes. Did you know it's very prevalent in the black community?" I asked, changing the subject, my stomach
stuffed from dinner and flipping through the television
to avoid eye contact with her.

"I'm in no mood to play games with you, Izzy. It
breaks my heart Rochelle and you are so distant. You
won't even let me tell you what's going on with her. God
forbid if I said anything to her about you. Izzy, you
know, she would be delighted to know you're attending
college classes."

"Grandma, I'm not trying to be upset because it's
Christmas. I just want to enjoy the day. Every time I think
about my mother and my father, the day in the church
basement feels like yesterday. After all these years, it
stills hurts that Mom lied repeatedly in my face about the
whereabouts and what was going on with my father. As
far as he's concerned, I have so much resentment in my
heart because he willingly missed out on my childhood.
Getting high in a drug-infested house with God-knows-
who was more important to him than me."

"Baby, listen to me and listen good. Your parents are
human too. They made mistakes and it's something you're
going to have to accept. I'm sure Shawn has looked in the
mirror at himself and face what he did to you. To be honest, yes, you are right, Rochelle should have told you
only when you were old enough to understand what was
going on. Maybe then you wouldn't be so angry. The day
in the basement, I'd never seen your eyes so red. I
thought—and I know I wasn't the only one—who thought
you were going to kill your father. I begged Rochelle
plenty of times to tell you but she didn't. She felt as
though shielding you from the truth was protecting you
from the pain and hurt. As far as your father, Shawn is a
changed man. I myself was very skeptical about him

moving back in with Rochelle, but he stepped up to the plate of being a husband. And yes, he has failed terribly as a father."

"Well, it didn't shield me but made it ten times worse," I said, sobbing.

"All I'm saying is that you've made Rochelle, your mother and my daughter, suffer for too long. Find in your heart to forgive both of them. Please, at least make amends with her at least before the Lord calls me home," she explained, rocking back and forth in her chair.

The month of January slowly went by. The money that I had managed to save was slowly chipping away. As a New Year's resolution, I ended all of my vehicle leases, only deciding to keep the paid-for Lexus and paid-off the Cadillac Escalade.

Luckily, Bernard passed the bar on the first try. He is currently working for E.L. Drummond and Associates law firm. Vera and him couldn't be more happy. All their hard work and efforts had paid off. Now, she's eager to start paying off those high student loans.

Rachel, on the other hand, has been blowing up my phone, leaving voice mail messages, apologizing. I guess she didn't get the news flash that I don't care. Finally I decided to block her number. There's just some things you don't say, such as God is going to punish you. I have forgiven her, but I will never forget those words that came out her mouth. I'm better off with her not being my friend. Besides, the bottom line was she was using me, anyway.

Alicia, I haven't heard from her. She must be laying low after the stunt she pulled at the Radisson Hotel.

Today was Saturday, which meant cleanup day in my apartment. Just as I was about to pour Comet all over the tub, the telephone rang.

"Hello?" I answered.

"Izzy, it's me, Opal, darling. Pack your bags, I'm taking you on a trip for at least a month. Be ready by tomorrow morning, my driver will pick you up. As far as today, I need you to come down to the office, right away, please."

"Opal, I'm excited about the trip. Where are we going?"

"It's a surprise. Now, get down here, please."

"Can it wait? I was just about to clean—"

"No, Izzy, it can't wait. I'll see you in twenty minutes," she insisted and hung up the phone.

"What's going on?" I asked, finding Opal overlooking tax documentation.

"Here, I want you to have this. I'm not taking *no* for an answer," she announced, handing me an envelope. I eagerly opened it.

"Did the tax audit go well?" I inquired.

"Yes, it went fine. It turns out the Internal Revenue Service owes me money," she giggled.

"Opal, this is the deed to the office building. I can't accept this," I said, almost in shock.

"You can and you will, darling because I transferred it over to your name. Now run along and get ready for our trip. I'm taking you home with me to see Naples."

"What kind of clothes should I pack?" I asked.

"The weather this time of year can be unpredictable. The temperature is around fifty degrees. Make sure you bring a coat, scarf, and gloves."

The next morning, Jimmy, Opal, and I boarded the Delta flight. He hadn't left Opal's side since the day he found me in the Radisson Hotel. I was truly excited about meeting most of her family. After leaving the office, I went to BankFIRST to place the deed in my safety deposit box. I also made two copies of it to place in my private vault in the apartment.

Upon arriving there it was foggy. I was greeted by her mother, father, and the rest of the family. They spoke some English but mostly Italian. Her relatives were doing double takes at me realizing I did look like Carmen. The house was more like a huge mansion, consisting of ten bedrooms, eight bathrooms, and a massive kitchen. Opal gladly gave me a brief tour of the house. In each bedroom, living room, dining room or study room, there hung pictures of the family. Each picture told a small story in their lives. For example, there was a picture of Opal learning how to swim. She appeared to be around five or six years old. The butler showed me to my room. Exhausted from the flight, I decided to take a nap.

"Wake up, Izzy, dinner is ready," Opal whispered while gently caressing my hair.

"What are we having?" I asked and yawned.

"A little bit of everything: antipasti, spaghetti, bread, veal and chicken marsala. I'm going to pour the wine for everyone," she stated, heading out my room.

"I'll pass on my glass. Lately, I've been having terrible headaches after I drink it," I admitted.

After dinner, Opal and Jimmy announced that they were getting married, right away. To be exact, the special ceremony would take place in the backyard on Friday. These two lovebirds didn't want to waste any more time. I was so excited that I couldn't stop crying tears of joy and excitement. Opal was a second mother to me. I will always cherish the friendship that we had. She never once judged and always let me make my own decisions.

The days that followed, Opal took me everywhere to see the sights and sounds of Naples. We visited the Museum of Royal Palace, the National Archaeological Museum, and the Museum of the Work of Santa Chiara. I picked a couple of bottles of wines, to take back home with me. Plus, I collected plenty of souvenirs that were hand-carved items from the Sorrento shopping street. Also, we hopped on a ferry to take us to the island of Capri to do more shopping. Most of all, I enjoyed going to the Pompeii's Amphitheater, which is huge. Opal and I got our daily exercise walking around it.

Friday had quickly come. I didn't want to leave because I was enjoying myself. Plus, it felt as though I just got here. The ceremony was elegant and simple just like Opal's style. She wore a mermaid-style gown that featured a shoulder strap. What do you give to a woman who has everything? I settled for a box of her favorite Godiva chocolates and a cruise for Jimmy and her.

Later on in the evening, after the last bottle of wine was opened and all the guests had left, I found myself in my room looking out the window, waiting for the sun to set when I heard a light knock on the door.

"Please come in," I answered, packing my clothes, hoping it would be Opal's seven-year-old niece. She secretly smuggled biscotti out of the kitchen and was gracious enough to share it with me.

"Hey, darling," Opal answered, coming into my bedroom with Jimmy. Still, Opal looked happy but she was even more pale than the last time I noticed. Figuring she was excited and now tired from the wedding, I didn't want to say anything to kill her joyous mood.

"Sit down, Izzy. We need to talk to you," Jimmy requested.

"Okay." I nodded and sat on the bed.

"I have liver disease. The late-night drinking has caught up with me. To be honest, I drank to ease the pain of missing Jimmy. A silly way to cope with my emotions, I realize now," she explained. I burst into tears and gave her a hug.

"Is there anything the doctors can do?"

"No, it's too late. I may have three more weeks to live. I'm dying, Izzy. The rest of the family doesn't know. If I would have told them as soon as I got here, the wedding ceremony wouldn't have been so happy. These last few days have been heaven to me. Sure, I have regrets such as not reuniting with Jimmy sooner and should have stopped the smoking and drinking. Please, don't cry for me."

"I can't help it. What am I going to do without you?" I sobbed.

"Be happy for me. My life has come full circle. I came here to Naples, my home, to die," she insisted, handing a box. Inside was a necklace with an oval-shaped locket with a picture of her.

"Thank you," I said, in tears.

"Dry up those tears.

"You're being taking away from me," I sighed.

"This is a joyous occasion. I have my family, Jimmy, and you here. How better can get things get? Now, I have a few requests."

"Opal, do we have to do this now? I feel as a truck has run over my heart."

"Yes, we do and please listen to me."

"I'll try my best," I answered, barely cracking a smile.

"The office building is yours to have. The other escorts want to make arrangements to buy it from you. Do not ask for no more than four hundred and fifty thousand dollars—that is, if you want to sell the building."

"What do you want me to do?" I inquired.

"You've already gotten out of the escort business. Sell it and take the money to purchase a home for yourself."

"All right," I nodded, wiping the tears from my eyes.

"Those ladies are not prepared to pay anything else. Also, in my will, I have set up a trust fund for your future child or children. My lawyer in Norfolk will be contacting you, soon. If you decide not to have children, when you turn forty, five hundred thousand will be passed on to you. The house in Oceanview was sold yesterday. The proceeds of it have already been wired into my account. For now, I'm just going to enjoy my life with Jimmy. He's got plenty of money, so we're bound to have lots of fun," she said, handing me a copy of the will.

"Anything else?"

"Don't squander my money away. Find your one true love and never let him go like I did. Most importantly, make amends with your mother and father. These are my requests and I expect them to be filled, Isabel," she proclaimed, holding me even tighter.

"I promise that I won't disappoint. I will fulfill your requests. I feel bad I'm the only one that knows of your health condition. When are going to tell the rest of the family?" I asked.

"I don't know, yet. What I am sure of is I have the right to die the way I want. My family would want me hooked up to plenty of machines in a hospital. I don't want that. Tonight, we're leaving to go to Paris. Please, always remember that I love you," she explained, kissing me on the cheek. She hugged me one last time before leaving the room.

Chapter 41

Five weeks had passed. The real-estate closing of Opal's—I mean, *my*—office building only took about forty-five minutes. The other ten escorts were excited to own the building and start making even more money. They gave me a few details of the reconstruction that would be under way. I, on the other hand, was given a cashier's check for four hundred and fifty thousand dollars. It was no more or less than what Opal requested.

She died yesterday. Opal decided not to tell her family, after all. Lately, I've been in the most depressive state, not wanting to eat or drink anything. Today, I made a stand to regain my life. It's what she would have wanted and what I definitely need to do. This morning I took a nap and dreamed Opal came into my bedroom and slapped me across the face, hard. "Snap out of it. He's coming for you, soon," she kept repeating. I woke up in a cold sweat.

After two more months of looking in thirty houses for the right one, Opal's agent, Ms. Parker, put in an offer at Creekstone Estates, a new development in the Kempsville section of Virginia Beach off of Providence Road.

Built with gray brick, the house is sturdy. It consists of four bedrooms, four bathrooms, living room, dining room, a huge kitchen, study room, and a two-car garage. The backyard needs some work but it's nothing a land-scaper can't touch up. A swimming pool and a Jacuzzi would be nice, but I'm in no rush. Not to mention, above the garage can be considered an extra bedroom, if needed. *Now, all I can do is wait,* I thought, *tapping on my fingers, looking at the* Kings of Comedy *on DVD.*

Another three days had passed. My offer of three hundred thousand was accepted. Plus, I was given a 20-percent discount because I was paying cash. Next, I got on the phone with K.L. Poole, a well-known and afford-able interior designer in the area. We spoke several times on the phone. I was very clear in what I wanted. Ms. Poole even went with me to pick out the furniture at Grand Furniture. My old furniture was sold to a young couple who was moving into my old apartment. With lit-tle money to spare, I didn't charge them a lot.

Today, I had an appointment with a financial advisor, Collin Taylor, at BankFIRST. He explained to me that I needed to diversify my money. With that being said, I put twenty-five thousand into a variable annuity, fifteen thousand into a 5-percent yield certificate of deposit, four thousand into an individual retirement account, and ten thousand into a money market account. Over time, I will contribute more to my retirement.

"The house is beautiful. Your mother would be proud," Grandma Elaine suggested as we were riding in the car. Today, she's showing me how to make her world-famous macaroni and cheese. I can cook but it would take twenty years of experience before I can even com-pete with her.

"Thanks, Grandma," I responded.

"No, thank *you*, baby."

"What are you thanking me for, baby?" I inquired.

"Thank you for making the right choice and for getting out of the gold-digging business. It has aged you some but I hope finally in your thirties you can get your act together and start some legitimate money. Besides this house, I hope you put away some more of *that* money."

"How did you know?"

"I can tell. It was either a new man or the oldest profession in the book. Izzy, I'm not here to judge you. I just want you to make the right choices and not—"

"Suffer the consequences," I blurted out, cutting her off.

"Before we go back to the house, do you mind stopping by Starbucks? I have got a taste for the espresso roast," Grandma suggested, changing the subject.

"Sure, no problem," I giggled.

"Girl, what are you laughing for?"

"Oh, nothing, you're drinking Starbucks. I thought you were a die-hard Folgers coffee fan. Plus, you joined the gym. Grandma, you're moving with the times. I never imagined to see the day. You've shown me old people are not always set in their ways."

"That's right, honey. There's nothing wrong with learning new things. I hope your hands are ready; because, you and I have to make six hundred chocolate chip and sugar cookies for Easter. Handing them out in the neighborhood, all these years, has become a tradition for me."

When we arrived inside, I noticed a sign that read BUSINESS FOR SALE. Luckily, the owner was there. After shaking his hand to greet him and inquiring about the business, he informed that he was leaving the area to be closer to his ill parents in Michigan and had no plans of coming back here to the Hampton Roads area. For a mere eighty thousand dollars, he was willing to sell me the business to get it off his hands. He was in a hurry to get out of town. Once outside the building, I quickly dialed Jimmy Risoto's phone number. I pitched to him the idea of him letting me borrow the eighty thousand dollars from him. He agreed as long as I could show proof of buying the business and monthly deposits going into the business account. Jimmy offered the money to me as a gift but I insisted to pay him back. The money would be wired into my account in two days.

With Opal's lawyer helping me with the necessary paperwork, I was the proud owner of a well-known coffee shop, hoping the money would be raking in. It is located between the intersection of Virginia Beach Boulevard and Independence Boulevard. As an added bonus, this one had a drive-through. Not wanting to put all my eggs in one basket, I opened a business checking and business savings account with Wachovia bank. My business and personal affairs, I wanted to keep separate. Plus, at the time, the bank was running a discount promotion. I was given three monthly charges of fees waived through merchant card services. Nowadays, people don't carry a lot of cash on them. Credit cards, check cards, and debit cards are vital to the survival of my business.

To celebrate my newfound business venture, I threw away in the garbage every piece of panties, G-strings, sex toys, thongs, corsets, and bras that I used on my former men. I'm on my way to Lynnhaven Mall to the Victoria Secret's semiannual sale to rack up on new lingerie, panties, and bras.

Each room in the house had a different color and decor. In the living room, study room, and kitchen, I chose bright colors to wake me up. In the bedrooms and in the bathrooms, I chose dark colors to relax me. After Ms. Poole's job was done and the furniture trucks pulled out of the driveway, it was just me standing in the foyer. I turned around and decided to take pictures of everything. This is the beginning of a new chapter in my life and I was going to embrace it. I'm heading into the right direction, making wise choices and I hope some good comes out of it.

Chapter 42

Grandma advised me that once owners and managers change so could the attitudes of the employees left standing with many unanswered questions. The first and obvious one is why? To my advantage, the previous owner did explain to them why and when he was leaving. Next, were the uniforms going to change? The uniforms would stay the same, with wearing black and their infamous Starbucks aprons. To gain their respect and loyalty, I had a one-on-one meeting with each of them. I introduced myself and wanted to get to know their personalities. The team consisted of four men (Cole, Justin, Randolph, and Martin) and four women (Marcella, Pam, Brittany, and Heather) with various age differences from sixteen to thirty-six. The same night the coffee shop was handed over to me was the same night I had Molly Maid Cleaning Service Company come in with ten workers to sparkle up the place to have a new shine. Their money was well-earned. I ordered the *Virginian Pilot, Daily News,* and the *New York Times* to be viewed. Also, I ordered magazines ranging from *Fit Pregnancy* to *High-lights for Children* to *Fishing*. With twelve magazines, I hoped to spark the interest of all age ranges coming into Starbucks. For the first two months, I introduced myself to the clients as the new owner and watched as the employees worked. In addition to my first day there people coming at seven o'clock in the morning and two o'clock in the afternoon received their coffee free. Plus, I learned the Starbucks philosophy of coffee and each blend. In time and with repetition, I will learn the lingo and how to make to make each item offered on the menu like the back of my hand.

After a busy Saturday, I rounded up the team to surprise them with dinner at Captain George's, the ultimate buffet for the seafood lover. Marcella didn't like seafood. Instead, prime rib, lasagna, and baked chicken were alternatives that she did like. After we all pigged out for two hours, I announced to them that everyone would be receiving a dollar raise. In addition, I appointed Cole the manager. He had been there the longest and had the leadership style that I preferred. Cole wasn't a micromanager. He stood back and let them do their job. Even if you did mess up, he didn't jump down your throat or make you feel as small as a mouse. I'm into building relationships with people, not resentment. Sure, the payroll would go up but it was just a small price for their dedication and loyalty. To be honest, I faced the cold, hard truth: I needed these people to help me run the coffee shop.

One year later, business is booming. I'm bringing a profit of nineteen thousand a month. After payroll, rent of two thousand a month, and utilities, I brought home a little over ten thousand a month. Three thousand a month went to my personal 401(k) plan. One of the services the previous owner didn't offer was health and retirement benefits. I encouraged all of my employees to invest in the 401(k) plan. Also, I matched a dollar and twenty-five cents for every dollar they contributed, up to 7 percent.

To keep the morale high at the coffee shop, I recognized people monthly for their hard work and dedication with money and gift cards. I worked the busiest days of the week, Mondays, Thursdays, Fridays, and some Saturdays. In time, I grew to know the customers that came in.

"Morning, Eric, I can help you." I stated ringing up his order. It's been the same since he started coming in here six months ago. He looked like a loveable teddy bear with a brown beard and eyes to match. His cologne, Jean Paul Gaultier, sparked my interest to start noticing him coming in the coffee shop. Eric Henry Dickerson was the proud owner of Dickerson's Painting Company. Each morning, he came in here to get his day started.

"A caramel *macchiato* with two scoops of sugar."

"You can put the sugar in yourself," I insisted, looking at the long line of customers waiting to get served and looking down at their watches. Justin was on the register, as well.

"Could you put the sugar in for me, please?"

"Hmm, this one time, just so you can get out of the line and out of my face," I giggled.

"Ha-ha, very funny, pretty lady," he snickered, handing me a twenty-dollar bill.

"Have a good day," I replied, trying to hand him his change and the coffee.

"Keep the change," he insisted.

"No, that's all right. You need it more than me."

"Isabel, you're right, I do need it to save up to take you out on a date. Put in a cookie jar for safekeeping. Please," he pleaded.

"All right," I said, placing the money into an empty cookie jar.

"Have a good day," he said and smiled.

"You too," I responded. At first, I was mean to Eric when he first started coming in here. To annoy the customers in back of him and me, he would take at least twenty minutes to place an order, looking up at the selections.

"Good morning, what can I get you?" I asked, taking the next customer.

"One blueberry muffin, please," she replied.

"Would you like any of our coffee blends?"

"No, thank you. I don't drink coffee," she stated, handing me her check card.

"Okay," I responded, swiping her check card to pay for her order.

"If you don't mind me saying, you do resemble a patient of mine."

"Oh, really," I suggested, blowing her off a little, concentrating more on getting through the morning rush.

"She just delivered a baby girl, four days ago. I was her OB nurse."

"A baby girl. What's her name?" I inquired.

"The baby's name is Lauren. I'm Nya Gamden, by the way," she explained.

"My mother is too old to have kids. It was nice meeting you," I replied, giggling, handing her the muffin in disbelief.

"Well, maybe I'm mistaken, but generally, I don't forget a face. Have a great day," she offered.

"You too, Ms. Gamden," I replied.

"Izzy," Justin called.

"Yes?" I asked.

"Are you all right?" he inquired with concern in his eyes.

"Umm, I'm not feeling well. Take over for me. I'll be gone for the rest of the day."

"Sure, I hope you feel better."

Driving on Interstate 64 West to get to my grandmother's house, I anxiously wanted to know the truth.

"Is it true?" I asked, barging into my grandmother's front door.

"Girl, what are you talking about?" she asked while putting her coat on.

"Did Mom have a daughter recently?" I inquired eagerly.

"Yes, she delivered your baby sister named Lauren four days ago. I was going to tell you tonight when you came over here for dinner," she explained, smiling at me.

"Oh my goodness. I didn't know Mom could even still have babies," I replied to Grandma while giving her a great big hug. I began to cry, feeling bad for all the time that we had missed. Birthdays, Christmases, Easters, Thanksgivings, and New Years had all quickly drifted by. Mom was fifty-two. Lauren was definitely a miracle baby.

"Now's let go over to the house and see your brand-new baby sister," she announced. It's been over fifteen years since I stepped foot in that house. Now, I'm about to come to face-to-face with everything I've been so afraid of. Getting to know and establish a relationship with my new baby sister was more important than the fear of my parents hurting me over again. I never took the house key off my key ring. Fortunately, she never changed the locks. As I entered into the house, I found Mom rocking Lauren back and forth in the chair. When she spotted me, Mom smiled, continuing to rock the baby. My father was in the kitchen washing bottles.

"Isabel Preston," Mom called out, almost dropping the bottle of warm milk in her hand. She immediately came over to hug me after handing the baby to Grandma Elaine.

"My baby has finally come," she announced with tears in her eyes. My father stood there, speechless.

"I met your OB nurse and she told me that you had Lauren. After I heard the news, it made me realize life is too short to be angry. I forgive both of you, Mom and Daddy."

"We love you too," they both said in unison as we embraced each other for a hug.

"Make one promise to me, please," I requested.

"Anything, you name it," Daddy replied, wiping his eyes with a damp paper towel.

"Don't hurt Lauren like you hurt me. Get it right this time with her," I pleaded.

"We will." They both nodded.

"Izzy, you finding it in your own heart to forgive me and with the birth of my second baby girl, I've got a second chance to make things right," he announced, smiling.

"Now, can I please hold my little sister?" I asked with tears coming down my face. This is one of the most special moments in my life. A little baby sister, what a wonderful surprise!

"Of course, the baby looks just like you, Izzy, when you were her age," Grandma cooed to Lauren while gently placing her into my arms.

"She's so little," I responded as Grandma passed her to me to hold. Lauren too had a head full of hair. Her eyes, on other hand, were a light gray color. Still, she was going to be a knockout just like her big sister.

Vera and Bernard came over to see the new edition to the Preston family. That night, I shared with Grandma, Mom, and Daddy about the birth of Sophia. I showed them pictures of her as a newborn to her now as a member on the cheerleading team. While Grandma and Lauren went to sleep around ten o'clock that night, Mom, Daddy, and I stayed up till three in the morning catching up on the last fifteen years. Mom still can't believe that I had a daughter. Mom is still working at Sentara Leigh Hospital as an X-ray technician. Fortunately, she was able to quit her second job at Farm Fresh years ago. Daddy now counsels recovering drug addicts at Core Street Baptist School. He's been drug-free for fourteen years and counting, taking one day at a time. For the last thirteen years, he's worked for Chesapeake Bay, Inc., a company that makes steel.

Getting pregnant with Lauren at age fifty-two was a complete surprise to my parents. The fact I know Mom and Daddy were still having sex was a complete turnoff. Hugging and kissing was all right with me but nothing else. At times, I have wondered if I'm still going to be doing *it* at their age.

Chapter 43

"Izzy, how much is in the jar?" Eric asked, eager to know the amount.

"Give me a minute. I've got to go to the safe and count it," I teased while preparing his coffee drink. It took a while to count the money because it was stuffed to the rim of the cookie jar.

"You've saved three hundred twenty-six dollars and fifty-seven cents," I announced after counting for ten minutes.

"Is that enough to take you out?"

"Where are we going? I don't know if you're crazy in the head. We need to go to a public place." *Maybe, I should give him a chance. It couldn't hurt to have a little male attention. Plus, he's been coming in here almost every day faithfully. Eric has become part of my day. He could get plenty of laughs out of me. I had to admit I looked forward to seeing him. At first, it was the coffee bringing him in, now my coworkers and myself all know it's to see me.*

"Okay, that's fair to say. A public place is where we will go."

"Again, where are we going?"

"It's a surprise. Saturday, I'll pick you up in the F-one-fifty around two in the afternoon."

"Let me write down my address," I replied, jotting it down on a green decorated napkin.

"See you then," he said, taking the napkin.

"Eric, one more thing," I stated, coming from around the corner.

"Yes?"

"Happy birthday," I said, giving him a small hug.

"How did you know?" he asked with a huge grin on his face.

"You mentioned to Randy a while back your birthday was coming up soon and you happened to mention the date to him. Then, he mentioned it to me."

"Thank you, I'll see you tomorrow," he responded with an extra pep in his step.

Eric arrived at my house at two o'clock on the dot. As soon as he put the car in drive, I came out of the house with a lavender flower printed dress hanging slightly below my knees and brown sandals to match.

"Hey, you," I greeted him while locking the door with the key.

"Hi, Izzy—um, you look nice, but you can't wear that where we're going," he stated.

"Where are we going?" I inquired.

"Fishing down by the Oceanview area," he replied, rubbing his hands together while wearing a red T-shirt and pair of jean shorts.

"Let me change," I said with disappointment in my voice. Strolling through the zoo was more what I had in mind.

"What? You're not up for it? Don't tell me you don't want to get your hands dirty for the sake of nature?" he asked.

"I—"

"See, this is what's wrong with pretty girls with have long hair and tempting eyes. You're too good to roll your sleeves up and do a little bit of work," he explained, cutting me off and giggling.

"I was going to say I've never been fishing before you put your two cents in. I want to go, but first bring let me change my clothes," I replied, opening the front door.

"While you're at it, pack a bag. The outfit you have on can be for later."

"If we get to later," I shot back at him before going back into the house.

"Don't forget to pack deodorant. You and I both know how musty you were when you hugged me in front all of those people, yesterday."

"What people? You mean the two customers sitting down? One's eyes were glued to their laptop and the other was flipping through the sports pages of the *Virginian Pilot*. My coworkers don't count, they already know you like me."

"Yeah, right. Are you going to invite me in?" he asked.

"Now, why would I do that?" I snickered, closing the door. Once in my bedroom, I put on a light blue T-shirt with cache shorts and white Nike DC's. Then I packed a small bag that included a pack of hand sanitizers for the evening. On the way to the lake, things were quiet at first. Secretly, we kept staring at each other back and forth. Luckily, Eric couldn't catch me staring at him because I turned my head too quickly. He, on the other hand, was so obvious. Eric needed to be keeping his eye on the road instead of me.

"Do you have earthworms as bait?" I asked, wanting to break the ice. We were both nervous. This feels different than being across the counter from him in the coffee shop.

"No, I personally don't use them. Instead, we've got tiny fish and squid to use."

Once arriving at the boat, Eric had all the necessary cargo. For instance, a miniature refrigerator, life preserves that I immediately put on, first aid kit, sunblock lotion, snacks, sodas, water, and a cooler to put fish in. He was eager to show me how to use my own fishing rod and hook the bait on. Eric began to explain the authorized and unauthorized areas of where you could fish. Plus, he mentioned you are not supposed to be drinking alcoholic beverage while fishing. The fish police didn't have a problem giving out tickets. Luckily for him, he didn't have to sneak beers and wine coolers, because he didn't drink.

"So, how long have you been painting?" I asked while we waited for the fish to make a move and applying the sunblock lotion to my skin.

"Fifteen years and I love it. Business has been good to me. Plus, the guys I have are hard workers. A job that could take a month we could get done in three weeks. What about you? You like the coffee business?"

"Yeah, I do. The opportunity and the money were there for me to buy Starbucks from the previous owner," I responded while placing a little bit of sunscreen on my face and then handing it to him.

"Nah, I don't need any sunscreen," he stated. "What were you doing before then?"

"Working here and there but nothing concrete. How are the kids doing?" I asked, changing the subject while putting a dollop of lotion in my hand and applying it to my arms and legs. Eric liked to watch as I slowly rubbed the lotion against my skin. Many years ago, I made a vow to myself not to tell any man what I did for a living. "Eric Junior is ten years old and my little man, Tommy, will be one next month."

"Where do you stand with the mother?" I inquired.

"We're been separated for five months. Things are going in the right direction so I should be divorced finally by May, next year. In the state of Virginia, when you have children, the husband and the wife have to be separated on paper for a year."

"If you don't mind me asking, why are two calling it quits?"

"We were high school sweethearts and grew apart over the years. Mirna and I don't have anything in common anymore and don't value the same things. The only thing we just recently agreed on was the kids. I love my boys to death. There's nothing I wouldn't do for the sake of their happiness. What I do value is being a father for them and taking care of home in all aspects. My own parents divorced when I was young. With me being the baby of the family, it took a harder toll on me than my two brothers and sister. Growing up, my dad wasn't there as much as he could have been. He remarried and took care of *her* kids. There wasn't enough room for my siblings and them too. I will not ever do that to Eric and Tommy. To spend even more time with them, I coach Eric Junior's basketball team and have lunch with Tommy at his day care three days a week. Anyway, she stopped believing in me with this business and my rental properties. Mirna wouldn't give me a dime to help start both of them. It hurts when someone you love isn't supportive. Giving up and failing wasn't an option so despite her nonsupport, I still continued with my dream of owning and operating my own business. It got to the point where we couldn't stand each other and resentment stepped in. Before it escalated to something else, I decided to take a stand for my happiness and end it. Soon after, she agreed. I deserve to be happy. Being miserable isn't easy to cope with. The house felt more of a prison. Plus, she always thought I was cheating."

"Were you? Before you answer, I want to let you know I won't judge you for the things you've done in the past," I stopped him. *I don't put anything past a man.*

"No, I wasn't. Being accused of cheating all the time, especially when I wasn't, gets old real quick."

"You are a big flirt, though."

"It's all harmless. Mirna took it to the next level, thinking I wanted the clerk at the gas station to the waitress at Red Lobster. We stopped being friends. She's goes to church five nights a week and my walk with God isn't as strong as hers. I'm a certified homebody and live just fine with my La-Z-Boy recliner seat, a glass of water in one hand and the remote control in the other. The next person I fall in love with, I want to be compatible with *her*. Enough about me. What's your story? Do you have any kids?"

"Yes, a daughter named Sophia who's eight years old living in northern Virginia. I gave her up for adoption because at the time I felt it was the best decision. It was one of the hardest decisions I've ever made. Her father received a seventy-year jail sentence for many counts of robbery and murder. I haven't heard from him since he got convicted," I explained, taking a deep breath.

"What's wrong? We don't have to talk about this if you don't want to," he explained.

"I'm all right, just haven't spoke about it in many years. Out of sight, out of mind, I guess. Getting back to the subject at hand, Bruce physically abused me during our seven-year relationship. Finally, I got up the nerve to stand up for myself. Beating him with the frying pan felt so good," I giggled, thinking twice about telling Eric I poured jalapeno juice and lemon in Bruce's face or about the rape, which I didn't tell anyone, including Vera. Plus, I didn't want to scare the man off.

"I don't understand how a man could hit a woman. The best thing to do is walk away before blows start flying. Good for you. Izzy, I'm proud you stood up for yourself."

"So tell me more about yourself. Where did you go to high school?" I inquired.

"I grew up in Norview and attended Norview High School. In fact, all my brothers and sisters did as well."

"I graduated from Lake Taylor, class valedictorian," I said, nodding.

"Get out of here. You're gorgeous and got brains. Anyway, keep going, I'm listening."

"Growing up, my life seemed perfect until Daddy didn't come home one day. The day turned into ten years. He was a crack addict. My mother knew where he was the whole time but wouldn't tell me even when I was of age to comprehend. Recently, I just reconciled with them because I was so angry at both of them. It took a while but I realized having a lot of pain, anger, and hurt inside of me wasn't beneficial to me, so I let it go. Plus, I have a three-month-old baby sister named Lauren. In essence, she's the one good thing that came out of all of this."

"Wow, you've been through a lot," Eric insisted.

"Thanks for listening. It's a quality that I like."

"You're welcome," he replied.

"Plus, you seem like a good daddy, which is a plus too," I added.

"Thank you." He nodded his head.

"Besides, if you were not a good father, you wouldn't be sitting here with me," I stated, running my fingers through my hair.

"Can I touch your hair?" he asked. Since the day I met Eric, he always seemed to be intrigued by it. For a while, he always emphasized my natural beauty and hair.

"No, your hands aren't clean. You got to earn to touch me anywhere," I replied, brushing him off. Just as I was about to go get a 7UP from the cooler, I felt a tug on my fishing rod. "I think I may have something," I mentioned excitedly.

"Izzy, keep rotating the reel toward you," he repeated three times. My catch of the day finally surfaced to the top, still wiggling, attempting to break away from the fishing rod.

"It's a salmon," he announced.

We caught a total of five fish. Three of his and two of mine were placed in the cooler.

"Where to now?" I asked, wiping the sweat from my face. The sun had drained my energy.

"If you don't mind, back to my place off of Tidewater Drive because it's closer. We can get cleaned up there."

Eric had a quaint one-floor, two-bedroom house. Pictures of the boys were all displayed in the living room and his bedroom. For a brief moment, I stuck my head in the kids' room and noticed a bunk bed set and a wooden desk. I felt dirty and comfortable enough to take a hot shower, desperately wanting to get out my sticky clothes. While placing my clothes in a jumbo Ziploc bag, I noticed on Eric's dresser a picture of the kids, him, and his soon to be ex-wife, Mirna. I had to admit she had a great smile with a round face and brown eyes. Her hair was shoulder-length and looked to be around one hundred and sixty pounds. *She doesn't have nothing on me,* I thought.

Once I finished my shower, lotioned my skin, touched up the hairdo, sprayed perfume on me, and put on my clothes, I waited in the living room for Eric to get himself together. He used the hallway bathroom. As I was almost dozing off to sleep, he rescued me in the nick of time.

"Izzy, by the look on your face, you're tired and so am

I. Can we grab a bite to eat and go rent a few movies and come back here? I promise to keep my hands to myself. What are you in the mood for to eat?" Eric inquired.

"Sure, I'm in the mood for chicken wings and French fries."

"Chicken wings and French fries, it is. I know a place not too far from here on Little Creek Road called House of Wings. The owner and I grew up together," he stated, lifting me up from the couch.

When we got there, the line was outside of the door and there was nowhere to sit so we decided to get take out instead. It was a full house up in here tonight. The restaurant had a look of a sports bar with two forty-two-inch plasma television screens both tuned to ESPN. Once we got inside and placed the order, two empty seats were available at the bar. The wings came in different varieties such as house, mild, hot, honey barbecue, and teriyaki. Eric ordered a combination of forty wings with all the different flavors. Stopping at the nearest Blockbuster, we rented the movies *Life*, starring Eddie Murphy and Martin, and Derailed.

On arriving back at Eric's place, we wasted no time tearing up those wings. They were so good. I made a mental note to tell Vera and Bernard about that wing spot. For the next two hours, Eric told me funny stories about his childhood and about the painting. Another quality I liked him is that he could make me laugh. Since we both had seen the movie *Life* several times, we decided to watch the other, *Derailed* in the living room. The only move Eric tried was putting his arm around my shoulders and I let him. It felt good.

As Eric drove me home, I was sad the night was ending. I had a great time and ate some delicious wings. I couldn't wait for the next time to see him. Plus, after he walked me to the door, being a complete gentleman, he didn't try to kiss me, which made we want his juicy lips even more.

This is our fourth date. We have talked for hours on the phone. I even had to increase my anytime cell phone minutes to two thousand each month. My bill was extremely high, but Eric was well worth it. I picked him up in the Lexus truck, excited about taking him to the zoo. It was featuring two new tigers who just arrived a week ago. Eric opened the door before I could knock. I could tell he was feening for my presence as I was feening for his.

"Hey, Izzy," Eric greeted me and kissed me on the cheek.

"Hi," I said walking into the house and right into the living room.

"Are you ready to go?" he asked.

"Yes, but can we talk for a few minutes first, please?"

"Sure," he stated, joining me on the couch.

"Eric, I really like you. Umm, I don't know where this is going and I'm not trying to rush it. Before we continue this relationship, I've got to have some sort of security that you are getting a divorce. I'm not trying to come off being forward, but may I see your separation papers?" I asked with my palms sweaty. *In the next moment he could ask me to leave for having a lot of nerve coming up in his house with demands,* I thought.

"Izzy, I can understand you needing security before you enter into this. I like you a lot and love being around you. I don't know where this is going but all I want to do is follow the beat. So if it takes showing you the separation papers to ease your mind, so be it. Give me a minute, I'll get them from my bedroom. By the way, after we come from the zoo, let's stop by Ruby Tuesday. I've got a taste for their New Orleans seafood platter and a fresh tossed salad."

As Eric went to retrieve the papers, I let out a huge sigh of relief. He passed my test, plus the papers looked legit. Besides, his lawyer was Opal's lawyer. I made a mental note to give Mr. Alton a call to never ever utter a word to Eric about my past, including Opal.

Later on that night, I decided to show Eric the inside my house. He wasn't a deranged psychopath after all. With guys these days, a woman has to be careful. You never know what you're getting into.

"I really like the colors and the furniture you chose for each room. You've done very well for yourself, Izzy," he mentioned. I appreciated a man who wasn't intimidated by my success.

"Thanks, but I had a good friend of mine who specializes in interior design who deserves every ounce of credit to come in and work her magic. After several trips to Pier 1 Imports, Garden Ridge, and Target, she came up with the style of the house."

"Can I have . . . ?" Eric asked, stepping up to me. We were standing in the dining room. Before I could answer, I knew what he wanted and I was planning on giving it to him, tonight, a kiss. I closed my eyes and he gently held my face as my tongue touched his. Afterward, we stared at each other.

"Well, it's getting late. I've got to start a job at five o'clock tomorrow morning."

"Yeah, I need to get in the bed too. Duty calls me at six o'clock in the morning." The sexual tension between us was thick in the air. My nipples were hard. I was grateful to be wearing a light jacket so Eric wouldn't be able to notice. One thing is for sure, his dick is hard too. When he kissed, my hand gently brushed up against it. I had to inquire about the size of it just in case I wanted to put it to good use. Sure enough, his manhood was bigger than I had previously thought.

Chapter 44

At five months, Lauren was starting to crawl a little bit, cutting her teeth, and running a fever. The doctor said it was normal and to give her the recommended dose of children's Tylenol as directed. I packed wet baby washcloths in the freezer. Once frozen, I let her gnaw on them, as she wanted to ease the pain and soreness. My baby sister was dedicated in Core Street Baptist Church. It's been many years since I set foot in this church. When we all walked up to the pulpit for the congregation to pray for Lauren, I could hear snickers from the aisles, knowing I would not be able to live down that incident. Grandma Elaine was proud and honored to have her entire family back together with a new addition. When Mom and Dad were at work, Grandma Elaine would take on the role as a full-time babysitter.

As a gift, I started Lauren an account with the Virginia college saving's plan. Plus, I took my family, Vera and her husband, the pastor and the assistant pastor with their wives to Captain George's. Unfortunately, Lauren had to settle for beef with gravy, potatoes, peas and fruit medley, Gerber baby-food style. Grandma didn't miss a beat and ate as many crab legs as I did. Coming to this restaurant as much as I have, I should invest in their stock, I thought when I gave the waiter my credit card.

Chapter 45

After the coffee shop closed and the crew was gone, I stayed back to get a jump-start unloading the truck. Tomorrow, I didn't want to set foot in this place and needed a break to rejuvenate myself. With Marcella on medical leave due to a hysterectomy and Brittany dropping back down to part-time because she was attending afternoon classes at Virginia Wesleyan, I was working more hours. If our clientele continues to keep picking up, I'll be forced to hire another team member. There was a knock at the door.

"Hey, you, how did your day go?" I greeted Eric after unlocking the front door.

"The day went according to schedule. My workers and I will be done with a building in Suffolk tomorrow. How was your day?"

"Busy, as usual. A guy came in to order a coffee-blend decaf. He drank three-fourths of it and then decided he wanted a refund. He didn't get it. People trying to get things for free drinks irks me," I explained, shaking my head.

"Yeah, people will try to get over if you let them," he agreed.

"You're right about that."

"Izzy, I don't like you staying here late at night by yourself," he mentioned, changing the subject.

"I have the Brink's security system."

"The security system is unable to bring bodily harm to an intruder."

"It's what I got you for and my twenty-two caliber pistol," I snickered.

"Is that right?" he asked, coming closer to me.

"Yes," I confirmed with my hands on my hips.

"Then I'll take the job."

"Hmm, mmm, you can be my personal security guard," I replied, returning to stocking the bottom cabinets with the last bit of packs of coffee behind the counter. The new flavors I ordered came in as well. I was glad to see them because the customers were preordering it.

"Yeah, I'll take the job. What do you want me to do first?" he inquired.

"Go turn off the lights, please, and thank you. We can walk out the back door," I replied, grabbing my jacket, purse, and keys. Right before I placed the security code in the system to arm it, Eric gently grabbed me and pinned me to the wall.

"What are you doing?" I questioned.

"Searching you. Isn't that what security guards do?" he asked while rubbing his fingers through my hair all the way down to my ankles. Meanwhile, I teased him by bouncing my butt off his dick.

Eric turned me around for our tongues to lock around each other. We were moving all throughout the store in a tight embrace. We ended up back at the counter. He took off my apron and black sweater while I took off his pants and boxer shorts. I removed his shirt while he removed my tights and admired the mango-colored bra and thong set, while putting on a Magnum condom. Eric laid me down on the counter, removed my thong without hesitating to stick his tongue on my clitoris for a few minutes. I despised being teased but it made me want his dick even more. Two can play this game and the only winner will be me. To my advantage, a bottle of whipped cream was lying on the counter. Pouring a serving in my hand instantly got Eric's attention. Next, I lathered my pussy with it, never once losing distinct eye contact with him. Placing two fingers on my clitoris, I started playing with it. Slowly, I placed the whipped cream and pussy-juice-drenched fingers into my mouth. It drove Eric crazy.

"Spread your legs," he demanded while I squeezed my breasts together, playing with the nipples.

"You got to catch me first," I stated, attempting to get off the counter. Getting only about ten feet away, Eric caught me to place me back on the counter.

"Show me what your dick can do," I giggled. Eric nodded and held a tight grip to my legs while he entered into my pussy. Holding my legs up in a straight line, he penetrated me, starting with subtle thrusts to forceful penetrations. With my pussy being elevated, the intensity of his penetrations were exhilarating. The first orgasm is always the best and I came by myself. The second one we came together. Afterward, Eric lay on top of me, out of breath. Both of us were sweating and sticky. All I could think about was the next go-around and how no other man has made me come twice in a row.

"So, Izzy, how much do I have left in the cookie jar?" Eric mentioned. We both busted out laughing.

"I don't know, I haven't counted it lately. Besides, you don't have to keep putting money in the cookie jar. I'll go out with you for free, now," I confessed.

"Izzy, I want you to know something. You only shared a little bit of your relationship with me about Bruce. I know he hurt you physically, verbally, and emotionally. You got me now and if you give me a fair chance, I will give you a good life without the hurt and pain."

"Thanks," I responded, resting my head on his shoulders with my heart feeling safe in my hands.

Chapter 46

Three months later, Eric and I were inseparable. More importantly, he was my best friend. We had so much fun together doing absolutely nothing at all. Just to be around him and know he was in my corner was enough for me. I am love with Eric. Now, I was waiting for the right moment to say it. I met his entire family and hit it off with his sister, Vickie, very well. Eric met my family as well. Grandma Elaine was pleased to see me with just one man.

A week of Progresso soup, Halls cough drops, and many Aleve cold and sinus pills popped into his mouth weren't helping Eric's symptoms of fever, aches and pains, chills, and sinus congestion. Dragging him to the emergency room was the only remedy I knew once he told me his chest hurt as if someone was sitting on it at four o'clock in the morning. Plus, I wasn't able to get any sleep because his cell phone was ringing every ten to fifteen minutes. At first, it didn't bother me. Now, the calls were getting under my skin.

Waiting to get into a room was unbearable. I hope seeing the doctor wouldn't add on another two hours. While Eric was huddled in the chair with a thick blue blanket, I whispered into his ear.

"How do you feel?" I asked while rubbing the top of his head. He preferred when I did it, putting him into a relaxed mood.

"Terrible," he replied, grabbing the Kleenex tissue box from my hand.

"Antibiotics will help," I assured him.

"Something will have to help."

"I know what will give you some kind of comfort," I stated, handing him a card with the latest model of a four-door BMW on the cover. Inside were two crisp one-dollar bills.

"Thanks, Izzy, but what's the two dollars for?"

"It will go toward your down payment for your dream car."

"I bet you have worked hard to earn this," he snickered, holding it up.

"That's not all. I have something to tell you."

"What, baby, I would love to hear it."

"Eric, I love you."

"Izzy, I love you too," he replied, grabbing my hand. Holding the tears of joy wasn't easy.

"Eric Dickerson," the nurse called. He and I followed her back.

The nurse checked his temperature, blood pressure, chest, and other vital tests to help determine what was going on with him and how to possibly fix it.

"The doctor will be in shortly," the nurse assured us while walking out of the small but private room. I pulled down the zipper of Eric's jeans to reach into his boxers to pull out his dick.

"Izzy, what are doing? I'm sick and we're in a hospital. All you want to do is hump."

"There is a huge difference in making love and humping. I prefer to make love, Eric. Since I can't kiss you, I have no choice but to resort to other measures. Don't worry, the doctor always knocks before he or she comes in," I replied, pulling down my sweatpants.

"Girl, you are crazy."

"Shh and let me ride you," I instructed him, sliding my pussy on his dick and putting a cherry cough drop into my mouth. Eric and I stopped using condoms two weeks ago because both of us got tested for HIV. Well, the results came out negative. During the waiting period for the results, I get so nervous because you never really know.

Turning around the other way so my butt faced Eric, he began to sweat in excitement.

"Izzy, you got a fat ass. This feels good," he said, after smacking it.

"I second the motion," I whispered while riding him up and down slowly. Suddenly, I got off of his dick to kneel down and started to suck it with the cherry cough drop in my mouth. It made it even hotter in my mouth.

"I'm going to come," he announced. "Damn, Izzy, that's was just I needed," he stated and took a deep breath. Finally, Eric agreed to lay down on the hospital bed wrapped back up into his blanket. After another hour of waiting, the doctor came in to examine him especially to listen to the sounds of Eric's chest. With the results of his laboratory tests and his vital signs, he was diagnosed with a sinus infection. He was given antibiotics and a stern recommendation to take at least three more days off to get his strength back.

Chapter 47

Eric's family welcomed me with open arms. His little son, Tommy, looked like a miniature him. The older one, Eric Junior, tolerated me, which I can empathize with. Don't get me wrong, he has never been rude or disrespectful but doesn't say much. For me, that's all right. His parents are getting a divorce, which cannot be easy for an up-and-coming eleven-year-old. His sister Vickie and I have become even more close, only after knowing each other for a short period. She and I swap out books all the time. Vickie is a fast reader just like me, taking us about three days to read one single book. Eric's mother, two more brothers, and sister are a close-knit family. Something I craved growing up. Maybe, a little part of me is envious. Nowadays, I try hard not to dwell on the past but look forward to the future.

Today was the first time meeting the rest of the clan at his sister's house. Vickie was having a fish fry with whiting and catfish and a seafood bake consisting of steamed clams, mussels, oysters, crabs, and potatoes. I had a taste for clams and lobster dipped in butter and Old Bay seasoning. There, Eric mainly sat around and joked with anyone who came within five feet of him. His brother's girlfriend, Cynthia, was almost in tears because he was ferociously teasing about her feet in stiletto heels. Eric said her feet looked more like slabs of meat. As the night winded down, Eric and his siblings sat around the kitchen table as they told me stories about him growing up.

Throughout the day and the past two weeks, his cell phone was going off constantly. Now, it was time for me to say something. With no harm done thus far, I wanted to give Eric the benefit of the doubt.

"Did you have a good time?" Eric asked as while we stepped in the front door of his house.

"Yeah, I had a blast. Your family members are down-to-earth people. David, your cousin, was practically the life of the party bringing back the Electric Slide. So what's going on with your cell phone and house phone? Why are you getting so many calls late at night and now during the days?" I inquired, changing the subject, not wanting to beat around the bush and taking a seat on the couch.

"Mirna thinks I'm a bad father."

"Why? You love your kids."

"To be honest, I think she says it just to bring me down. She makes me second-guess myself. Part of it is I feel guilty about the divorce as far as the kids go. Eric Junior isn't taking it so well and he's acting out in school. The boy doesn't want to do his homework. I know how it feels not to have a father around. I don't want the boys to think I'm going to do the same. It would hurt deep down if Eric Junior or Tommy felt the same pain I felt growing up."

"The only way to do that is to make sure you're there.

Eric, you do that already. You're a great father. It's one of the qualities that I love about you," I stated. "Thanks, Izzy. Mirna is trying her best to get everything in the divorce. She wants both cars, the house, and wants *me* to keep making the mortgage payment for the whole life of the loan. Plus, she wants the four rental properties that I have. I would never leave her broke and destitute, so why is she trying to do the same to me? I have to live and maintain my life too. I'm trying my best to make it to the finish line of May and things hopefully will be final. By that time, the houses will be sold—all of them, including the one she lives in. After the sales, she can get her half and I can get my half. Then, I can fully continue to go on with my life. It kills me the fact she is entitled to half of the rental properties but refused to give me a penny to fix them up. My lawyer schooled me on *never* making that mistake again. See, Izzy, if I would have put them under a corporation, she wouldn't be entitled to anything. Mirna has got fifteen thousand in a money market account sitting at BankFIRST but you don't see her trying to get a penny of it or anything out of her four-oh-one-k plan. Now, she quit her job of nine years working for the government as a receptionist at the FBI building to go back to school. Now, I'm pretty much stuck with paying my bills and the bills where my children live. What's wrong, Izzy, why are shaking your head?"

"Why would she quit her job knowing ya'll are getting a divorce? I'm shaking my head because it doesn't make sense you have to pay all the bills. It's your money, though. At the same time, I see your logic partially. You pay the mortgage and utilities because it's providing a roof over your childrens' head and since Mirna lives there as well, she's reaping the benefits. On the other hand, on the outside looking in, she is using you to pay for everything and it isn't right. If you don't mind me asking, did you do something to Mirna for her to treat you this way?"

"No, nothing in particular. She and I were together were for convenience. Now, Mirna doesn't have me to fall back on and won't have me pay for everything come springtime and the month of May. She's pissed about it."

"Do me a favor, please?" I requested.

"Anything for you," he replied, stroking my hair.

"Please don't let me know what you go through with her on a daily basis spill over to our relationship. We have a good going here and I don't want it to go sour because you're so consumed with the divorce. When you met me, were you honestly ready to start dating?"

"Yes, but with you, it felt different."

"How so?"

"I didn't like you at first. You were stiff, didn't loosen up, and I couldn't get a smile out of you for nothing. Plus, you were extremely rude to me. I couldn't stand you."

"Why did you keep coming in?" I giggled.

"My philosophy is simple. I had to have something pretty to look at. Sure, there's another Starbucks five miles down the road, but the ladies in there are ugly. You, despite your bad attitude and terrible customer-service skills, you are still beautiful. Izzy, you're definitely my type. Plus, I love the fact you don't wear makeup. Natural beauty is what I prefer."

"I felt the same way and didn't like you either because you purposely took way too long placing your order. You irritated me and the people behind you."

"Hey, I had to get your attention, somehow." We both busted out laughing.

"I'm glad we talked."

"Me too," he replied.

"So, can you tell me which breast you want in your mouth tonight?" I asked while unbuckling his belt.

For the past two months, the tension between Eric and me was getting thick. The calls were getting worse and he steadily answered every time Mirna called. If she wasn't calling about the kids, why the hell did he have to answer the phone? Keeping the peace shouldn't come at the price that Mirna wanted. Eric couldn't see past her manipulative and controlling ways. The funny thing I couldn't understand is when I wasn't with him, then the calls stopped. One thing for sure was that Mirna is definitely miserable with her life and she wanted Eric to feel the same way. He had to stand up to her and there was nothing I could do about it. The only thing I could do is leave his ass because this was getting to be too much for me. Still, I did love him, though. Now, I looked forward to not seeing him because I knew I would get peace from hearing about their constant fights and disagreements. It was if I was in a relationship with her and him. Time and time again, I told Eric I didn't want to hear about the daily dose of drama Mirna was spooning to him. Now, I was on my way to pick up Eric from the job site off of Cedar Road in Chesapeake to take him to the Ford dealership on Military Highway. His truck was getting brake pads and four new tires.

Instead of greeting me, Eric was on the phone arguing with Mirna. What a typical day, I thought, shaking my head.

"What's wrong with you?" he asked, putting on his seat belt.

"Nothing," I spat back at him.

"Are we still on tonight for bowling?"

"Yeah, I guess."

"You sure you're all right, Izzy?" he asked again, try-ing to rub my ear. I quickly block my ear with my hand.

"Do you have to be on the phone with her all the time when you're with me?"

"I don't believe this. I've had a day from hell. Here we go again, with this," he announced, raising his hands up.

"Eric, really; you don't see me every day so the least you can do is cut down the phone calls to a minimum. I bet you wouldn't like it if the wheels were turned." I may just put my words to the test.

"Izzy, you're not going through a divorce so there's no reason for you to be on the phone with an ex-husband."

"Whatever, Eric. You still don't get it," I stated as we pulled up to the dealership.

"Are you coming in?" he asked. I didn't answer be-cause my actions spoke louder than words. I rolled my eyes, put my truck in park, and proceeded to get out.

"What do you mean, the truck isn't ready?" Eric asked the man behind the counter while still answering Mirna's every becking phone call after he entered the building. I resumed the position of flipping through magazines in the waiting area, so aggravated and irritated at Eric. Maybe I need to reevaluate this whole relationship. I feel as if I'm talking to a brick wall and it's driving me crazy.

"Sir, I do apologize, but we were unable to get to your vehicle in time. To guarantee the truck be ready by five o'clock, Mr. Dickerson, you were supposed to drop it off before eight in the morning. Unfortunately, you didn't arrive here until ten o'clock," he explained, looking at the paperwork.

"No one ever told me that I had to drop the truck off before eight in the morning. . . ."

"Let me see a manager, right now," I demanded while cutting off Eric. I had to blow off steam on somebody.

"Hi, I'm Peggy, the store manager. How may I help you?" she asked with an ever-so-sweet smile.

"No one ever told Eric the truck had to be dropped by eight in the morning. He cannot wait until the morning because he has a business to run just as yourself, Ms. Peggy Lumbard. What can you do to help us out? I would hate to have to take this matter to Mr. Brinson, the owner," I suggested after reading her name tag. *He was a former client of Opal's.*

"Yes, ma'am. We'll take care of this right away. Give me a half an hour and your truck will be right out, Mr. Dickerson."

"How did you know the owner's name?" Eric inquired. I could tell he was impressed with the way I handled things.

"When we came in the building, it states the owner's name on the door," I said with an attitude.

"Thanks for helping me out with this," he admitted.

"Hmm, mmm," I spat back, rolling my eyes at him with my arms folded together. Just as I was about to sit down, guess who came in the door.

"Eric, I thought you were coming to get the kids tonight?"

"No, Mirna, tonight is your weekend with the kids," he replied, shaking his head.

"It's your weekend," she stated. Mirna had another woman with her resembling a sister. They favored, but the sister was more on the slimmer side.

"How did you know I was here?"

"So, this is who you've been seeing?" she asked, completely ignoring his question.

"Who I see isn't your business, Mirna," he spat back at her.

"You'd rather spend time with her than your kids," she said, getting louder. People were starting to look.

It was a shame Mirna was using the kids to manipulate him. Why couldn't he see through it? No one better not say anything out of the way to me. Eric thought I was mean when he first strolled up into the coffee shop. He doesn't know what a beast I can be, if provoked.

"Stop making this about Izzy. You shouldn't be following me around," he stated.

"Oh, I all ready know her name. Vickie's niece, Deadre, told Mary and me all about you and her."

"You asked my thirteen-year-old niece about my business. Damn, Mirna, you were wrong for that," he insisted. I made a mental note to get on the phone and tell Vickie once I leave here about this.

"Eric, you're wrong for wanting to be with her instead of your own flesh and blood."

"For the last time, this wasn't my weekend. After I get the truck, I will be more than happy to pick up my kids for your weekend and mine."

"Mom, Dad, Tommy's diaper needs to be changed and there's no more in his bag," Eric Junior explained, stepping into the building. This was becoming a circus.

"Mirna, you left the kids in the car to come in here and degrade me like this?"

"Where else would be they be, you bastard? Eric Junior, come on over here and look at the reason why your daddy don't want spend any time with you." Eric Junior reluctantly came over.

"Excuse me, Eric, but if you havn't noticed, Tommy is in the car by himself. I have some leftover diapers in my car that he can have," I butted in, not wanting Tommy to be left alone in the car and not wanting him to be sitting in his own bowel movement. Mirna may be pissed at Eric for whatever reason, but she shouldn't be resorting to lies. Eric was a good father and spent most of his free time with his boys. He loves those boys more than his life. As I was heading out of the door to get the diapers, Mary pushed me in the chest and Mirna grabbed my hair and pulled it hard.

"You're not going near my baby," she ranted.

"Go back to the car with your brother. We'll be out in a minute," Eric instructed Eric Junior. He was coming toward us to get her off of me but I didn't want or need his assistance.

Instantly, the beast came out of me and I went into psycho mode while all these people were watching. By this point, I didn't care. Rummaging through my purse, I got out the Taser gun and shocked both of them on the shoulders, thighs, arms, legs, and face. Both of them fell to the floor. Next, I sprayed Mace in their faces. Mirna and Mary were screaming in agony.

"Izzy, that's enough. Stop it," he insisted, trying to get the Taser gun out of my hand.

"Don't touch me. Nobody ever touches me. Ladies, this is the year 2006; you can get killed for putting your hands on people," I announced. Eric backed up, not wanting to get a taste of what I had in my head. The man wasn't stupid. He already knew I was pissed at him for Mirna's ongoing phone calls and rants. The crowd of people in the waiting area starting to clap and cheer because they knew both sisters tried to tag-team me. "You are just mad because he doesn't want you no more, Mirna. This is between you and him. Leave me out of it. I bet next time, you'll think twice about putting your hands on Isabel Preston."

"I know that's right," a woman with three small kids shouted.

Next, I dialed the police because I was going to press charges on both of them. Luckily, they arrived in ten minutes. Mirna and Mary were still lying on the floor. Eric called Vickie, who worked only five minutes away from the dealership, to come and pick up the kids, which I was grateful for because they didn't need to see this. Plus, he didn't want child protective services to get involved for Mirna leaving a one-year-old in the car. Once back in the building, Eric was trying to apologize but I didn't want to hear anything he had to say. Not today or tonight. Out of the corner of my left eye, I spotted three police cars pulling up. I guess I wasn't the only one who called the police. When they came in, all of the police were in disbelief. While taking the names and numbers of all thirteen witnesses who saw the whole scene and clearly were in favor of me, I overheard the police chief being called on their intercom. After five minutes, a man who appeared to be in his late sixties walked inside the building.

"Mary, Mirna, why are you two on the floor?" the gentleman asked.

"Dad, we had a disagreement with the young lady over there," Mary confessed, but failed to go into detail.

"What happened?" he asked while shaking his head. It turns out one of the witnesses in the waiting area was an attorney and explained to Police Chief Birnes what happened. Based on what she explained and the rest of the statements from the other witnesses, Birnes had no choice but to arrest his own daughters. Both were handcuffed and rode away in the police car. Oh well, I didn't feel an ounce of sympathy for either one of them. The golden rule is to keep your hands to yourself. It's a damn shame your own father has to arrest you. Their father looked so embarrassed. Mary Birnes and Mirna Dickerson were charged with assault and battery and disturbing the peace.

An hour had passed and I had calmed down.

"What can I do to make things right?" Eric asked while I was walking to the door.

"Mr. Dickerson, your truck will be ready in fifteen minutes," the manager informed him.

"Thank you so much."

"To be honest, Eric, this really isn't your fault. But right now, if you want to make things right, leave me alone for a couple of days. Your drama with Mirna is becoming too much for me. I'll call you when I can," I stated and walked out of the door.

Eric couldn't leave me alone for an hour. Every hour on the hour he was blowing up my phone, leaving voice mails telling me how much he loved me. I went and stayed at Grandma Elaine's house to seek some relief from my frustration. After four days, I decided to talk to Eric. When I opened the door, in his hand were a popcorn set filled with Goobers, snow caps, Skittles, Sour Patch kids, two huge popcorn tins, ten packs of light butter and kettle corn popcorn, two eight-ounce glasses, and a fifty-dollar gift card to Blockbuster. I had to admit it brought a smile to my face. Eric really thought about this gift, which I appreciated. A piece of jewelry would have meant nothing to me. Also, he had a plastic bag, but I couldn't glance to see what was inside of it.

"Izzy, I know it wasn't my fault what happened, but I want to apologize, anyway. I'm going to take a stand against Mirna's antics; because I realize now, it may cause conflict in our relationship. She's my past and you're my future. I would rather focus on that. I don't know about you, but I'm looking forward to the future. You really touched me when despite everything going in the Ford place, you were still willing to help Tommy."

"The kids are the innocent victims in this situation. I would never mistreat a child because I wouldn't want someone to do that to Sophia, Lauren or anyone's kids for that matter."

"The phone calls are going to stop. You're right. We are not together twenty-four a day. I know you just want to enjoy the time we do have together."

"Is the divorce still going to be final in May?" I asked.

"Yes, I talked to my lawyer and told him what happened. Mirna cannot use this as an advantage with the divorce. Anyway, enough talk about that. I ordered your favorite pizza from Pizza Hut, meat lover's on thin crust with no green peppers, twice-baked chicken wings, and cinnamon sticks."

"What's in the bag?" I asked.

"There are mystery and romantic movies. I went to Wal-Mart and picked up a whole bunch of DVDs I think you will like."

"Thank you."

"So, are you just going to have me stand out here until the delivery guy comes? He'll be here in ten minutes, but before I keep resuming my post at the door, can I use the bathroom, please?"

"Sure," I giggled.

The court date was scheduled mid-October, fifty days from now. If Mary and Mirna were willing to leave me alone till the court date, then I would be willing to drop the charges. If not, well, someone else could be paying them a friendly visit. One thing Opal taught me was to stand up for myself. I wasn't willing to back down now.

Chapter 48

Thirty days and counting, Mirna gets bold enough to leave a voice mail on my house phone.

"You know, it wouldn't be so bad if I didn't love my husband, but a woman can only take so much. I'm going to leave it in God's hands. You're not the first one. I've been down this road with my husband before. I love my husband and I know he loves me. I'm not going to call you any more," she explained. Then, the phone hung up.

On the day of court, I played the voice mail for the judge, who didn't find it funny at all. Dressed in a black pantssuit with low black heels and a matching pearl earring-and-necklace set, I truly looked innocent. Eric and I thought it was best that he didn't show in court. All I wanted was a restraining order to be put on both of them. Just in case in the future they wanted to act up, I had a camera system built into the coffee shop just in case they want to come to my place of business. The system will record each person coming in out of the coffee shop and also the cars riding by. I didn't think those two would dare come to my house, though.

"Ms. Birnes, let me see just say that you need to stay out of your sister's affairs. This is what clearly landed you here. Mrs. Dickerson, you are the first and you won't be the last of a woman going through a divorce. Yes, you may be upset that Mr. Dickerson may or not be diverting his attention to Ms. Preston, but it doesn't give either of you the right to put your hands on her. I am granting the restraining order request. I don't want to see Ms. Birnes and Mrs. Dickerson in my courtroom, anymore. Next case," the judge proclaimed.

One month later

"Can I talk to you for a few minutes?" Pam asked as we were setting up in the morning at the coffee shop.

"Sure, what's on your mind?" I asked with concern.

"Well, we've been getting a lot of calls with people hanging up."

"Did you look at the caller ID?"

"Yes, but it either comes up restricted or unknown."

"Pam, thanks for letting me know. I'll take care of it," I responded, making a mental note to get in contact with Verizon to see if there's a way I can find out who's calling and hanging up. *What childish games people play*, I thought.

"One more thing," she insisted.

"Yes?"

"Yesterday, around three o'clock in the afternoon, I got a call from someone who asked is there's disciplinary actions on an employee fraternizing with a customer?"

"Was this person a she or he?"

"A woman and she sounded pissed."

"What did you tell her?"

"I told her no," she replied with tears in her eyes.

"What's wrong?" I asked, giving her a napkin to wipe her eyes.

"I've been so stressed-out."

"What's been going on? I have noticed you've been somewhat distracted lately. I figured you were stressed-out about school. Pursuing a degree in chemistry isn't easy,"

"Well, that's the problem. It's school. I've been having tutor sessions with my organic chemistry professor. Last week, his wife stormed into the classroom and threatened to go to the dean because she thinks we're having an affair; but we're not. What if I get kicked out of school? My parents will disown me. I've worked so hard to maintain my three-point-oh grade and you're right, it's not easy," she sobbed even harder.

"First of all, you're not going to get expelled. If she doesn't have any proof, then there's nothing she can do. Even if she does, it's her word against yours. Her frustration and anger needs to be directed to herself or the professor. So you think she was the woman that calls because she has or had been coming in here to get coffee?"

"Exactly."

"First of all, Pam, I am the owner of this coffee shop and I reserve the right not to serve anyone if I choose not to. If she does decide to come in and make a scene, we'll simply call the police. Picking a fight with a nineteen-year-old isn't cool. Don't worry, good always prevails over evil."

"Thanks, Izzy, for being there for me. I guess I needed to vent."

"No problem, we'll keep this conversation between us," I said, hugging her. The professor's wife wasn't behind this. *It was probably Mirna and I was ready for her if she decided to come to my place of business,* I thought.

Later on that day, Mirna Dickerson comes strolling into the coffee shop demanding to be served and of course making a scene. When I told her to leave, she spray-painted the words *home wrecker* on the window. Within thirty minutes, I had a cleaning team come out to clean the window off. Now, she's crossed the line again and in violation of the restraining order. Plus, this was getting old. Luckily, I jotted her license plate number and called the police. Also, not one customer was in the shop to see what went down. Losing business was the last thing I wanted. The Virginia Beach police picked her up at a near-by grocery store with the kids in the car. Eric was able to get the kids and take them back to his house. Mirna and her antics were not going to get the best of me. Now, I knew it was time to pay a visit to my little friend.

"Isabel, it's so good to see you. How are you holding up with Opal being gone?" Mayor Smith asked. He had been the mayor of Norfolk for the past ten years.

"Mr. Smith."

"Call me Nathan."

"Okay, Nathan, I take it day by day with the death of Opal. I miss her so much but I know she will always live on in my heart."

"Yes, she was some kind of lady and the first person to ever give me campaign money."

"Opal always spoke highly of you, as well."

"So, Izzy, what brings you down here? This must be serious by you gracing me with your presence."

"Well, I've been having a few problems with your police chief's daughter, Mirna Dickerson. This is all stemming from the divorce of her soon-to-be-ex-husband, Eric, who is my good friend. All of her anger and frustration is being directed toward me and I would hate to have to resort to *other* measures. Maybe, you can talk to him so he can talk some sense into her."

"Wow, if Opal was still alive, this woman wouldn't have a job, house or car. She really knew how to stick it to the ones she didn't particularly care for."

"Mirna even came into the coffee shop acting stupid. Now, she's at the Virginia Beach police station waiting to be booked."

"Let me handle this," he insisted and dialed the phone, leaving it on speakerphone.

"Chief Birnes," a voice answered.

"Byron, how are you, this is Nathan."

"Hello, Nathan, how are you doing?"

"I'm great. How is it going down at your station?"

"Things couldn't be better. So what can I do for you?"

"Well, your daughter, Mirna, is bothering a good friend of mine. I need to have it stopped instantly. This good friend is pretty much family to me, Byron. Well, I consider you part of the Norfolk family as well and I want you to continue to be part of the family. Your daughter is causing a lot of trouble. Can you do my friend and me a favor and talk to your daughter about the importance of being part of the family?"

"Nathan, I sure will."

"Thanks, Byron, I really appreciate it. Your performance evaluation is due next month. Looking good so far and let's keep it that way."

"All right, Nathan. I'll be definitely talking to you soon. I've got a few phone calls to make," he insisted and hung up the phone.

"I don't think she will be bothering you anymore," he stated.

"Thanks, Nathan," I replied, shaking his hand and

leaving a one-hundred-dollar gift card from Golf Galaxy on his desk.

The second court date was quickly moved up to the following week and the same judge was handling the case.

"Mrs. Dickerson, I'm sorry to see you back here. After hearing the testimony of the Starbucks coffee shop employees, viewing the camera tape of you in Ms. Preston's place of business, and me seeing you for the second time, I have no choice but to sentence you to thirty days in jail. If you do happen to grace my courtroom again, I won't be so nice. You are literally wasting the court's time. Have fun in jail," the judge stated with sarcasm.

"Are you all right?" Bernard asked as we were leaving the courtroom. Vera and him thought it was best if I was represented by an attorney. I offered money for his time but he refused to take it.

"I'm fine. Thank you for asking," I assured him.

"Ms. Preston, can I have a moment of your time?" a man's voice asked.

"I'm in a hurry but I can spare a few moments," I responded, looking down at my watch.

"Don't you dare ask me to leave. Vera will have my head. Besides, just in case Birnes gets out of line, you have a witness," Bernard whispered in my ear.

"First of all, I just want to apologize from my wife and me. This situation has become a thorn in both of our sides," he confessed, shaking his head.

"I appreciate your apology," I replied, eating this moment up.

"Let me assure that there won't be outbursts from Mirna. I usually stay out of my childrens' affairs but when it slides over to me, I have no choice but to get involved.

"Give Mayor Smith my best."

"I certainly will," I mentioned. Too much time, energy, and the taxpayers' money had already been wasted.

Chapter 49

"Hello?" I answered my cell phone.

"Hey, baby, it's me. Whatcha doing?" Eric inquired.

"Lauren and I are watching television, the Sprout Channel. She loves to look at Dora the Explorer. I have her for the weekend. Mom and Daddy went to Myrtle Beach in South Carolina because of a teachers' convention. Come over when you can, dinner is almost ready."

"I'm on the way with my little man."

"Great, now Lauren can have a playmate."

The doorbell rang.

Tommy greeted me with a hug and an Oreo cookie. He was getting bigger and bigger each time I saw him.

"What's for dinner?" Eric asked, putting Tommy down and picking up Lauren to greet her.

"Did Tommy . . . What is that on your forehead?"

"What do you mean?" he questioned, going into the refrigerator, reaching a bottle of Welch's grape juice.

"Eric, you know what I mean. Why are there stitches on your forehead?"

"Mirna got out of jail yesterday, after serving almost four weeks. I went over to drop the kids to her. When I got inside and the kids were out of sight playing in their rooms, she hit me with a flower vase."

"You have Tommy so where's Eric Junior at?"

"Mirna's other sister came and got him so he could spend some time with his cousin who's around the same age as him."

"Is your head going to be all right? Do you think the kids could have seen what happened?"

"Yes, my head will be fine in a few days. No, the kids were upstairs. If anything, all they heard was Mirna screaming. She's blaming me for everything. Mirna said cousins she didn't even know about were calling, telling her to back off of you. The mayor of Norfolk called her father on the charges you pressed against her. Indirectly, the mayor threatened his job if she didn't stop. Mirna's father is the head of the family and heavily depended on. He brings home well over one hundred and fifty thousand dollars. None of her sisters and brothers are speaking to her so she's taking her anger out on me. Izzy, it took all of me not to hit her back, but for what, that's what she wants. Now and going forward when I pick up the kids, I will take Vickie or my brother with me as a witness. It goes to show this is a small world. There's no telling who you know," he explained, shaking his head.

"Did you know the mayor was going to say something?"

"No, perhaps the mayor stumbled onto the case."

"Izzy, no one accidentally stumbled onto it. Someone must have said something."

"Well, years ago I used to babysit for the mayor and his wife. Perhaps his wife, Mrs. Smith, could have said something to him and the rest is history. The first time we went to court, I ran into her in the hallway. When I told her why I was in court, her face didn't look too happy. Hopefully, Mirna will get the picture and leave me alone," I explained, feeling a little bit guilty for lying to Eric, but there's no need for him to know everything.

"Me too because the situation is getting too serious. The choice is up to her."

"Did Tommy eat?" I asked, changing the subject.

"Probably not."

"Let me feed both of them, give them a bath, and put them to sleep. Meanwhile, can you watch the tomato sauce?"

"Yeah, can you trust me enough to fix the noodles?"

"Yes, I trust you, enough," I stated.

"I know you like the noodles, hard," he reiterated.

"I'm starving," I announced, coming down the stairs. The kids were fast asleep. Their tummies full and a warm bath always does the trick of sending them to la-la land.

"Come in here and eat," he instructed. Eric had the table in the dining room set up with two candles. The CD of the R&B group Floetry was playing in the background. My favorite song, "Sometimes U Make Me Smile," was on.

"I love you so much, Izzy," Eric proclaimed, taking a bite out of his meatball.

"Why?" I inquired.

"Because you're you. I love you just the way you are. You're a good person and make me look forward to the next day. You taught me what love is really about. Love is putting that person first before you at times. Your love is not selfish or judging. Izzy, you have done that for me time and time again. Plus, you're not needy. You don't need me or any man, for that matter. But you've found in your heart to love me. I know I'm not the best to be around. I know I get on your nerves now more here lately than before and you think I'm not listening to you but I really do listen. With a thriving business and much success to come, you've set the foundation of your years to come and your future children."

"Thanks, Eric." *I needed to hear that,* I thought. "I love you too. The business is going well. I've been thinking about up opening up a Quiznos sub restaurant."

"In which city?"

"I don't know, maybe Norfolk or Chesapeake. It's nothing written on paper, yet. We'll see what happens. I'll talk to the bank in the next coming weeks. How's work for you?"

"Izzy, I got so many jobs that I can't handle everything. When people call me for jobs, I can't say no because I don't want to lose that almighty dollar. You see how much I pay out in bills a month. I hired three more guys because I'm not going to work myself to death," he said, twirling his spaghetti.

"I understand what you're saying. Once you sell the house she lives in and sell the rental properties, those mortgage payments will be obsolete," I explained with one last bite of spaghetti.

"Yeah, you're right. What's for dessert?" he asked, buttering his baguette.

"You know, I consistently have sweets in the house."

"Why do you think I come over so much?"

"To see me, of course, and you're going to be my sex slave."

"Nah, somebody lied to you. I come here to see Little Debbie, Breyers, Blue Bunny, Snickers, and Hershey's."

"Tell Little Debbie, you're my man. It would be unfortunate if she got smooched." We both started laughing.

"So what do you have?" he asked, going back to the first question.

"I got a chocolate cream pie in the refrigerator."

"Sounds good."

"To make it even better, I drizzle whipped cream on the top with cherries."

"Isabel Preston, we got the whole weekend to ourselves. What do you want to do?"

"Let's stay in for the weekend. Besides, it's supposed to be rainy and in the forties. I don't want either of the kids getting cold."

"You want kids, Izzy?"

"Yes, someday it would be nice. Don't get me wrong, I will treat Tommy and Eric Junior as if they were my own but having my own is scary."

"Well, you're getting much practice with Lauren. The little girl loves you and you do pretty well with her. I mean, child protective services hasn't been called out," he laughed.

"A daughter would be nice," I suggested, picking up his plate and mine.

"Are you up for chess, tonight?" he questioned.

"Yes, but I have to warn you that I'm going to beat you. Before we get started pick your lip up from off the floor," I joked.

Chapter 50

Planning a getaway weekend was easy as a click of a button. In Williamsburg, Virginia, which is about an hour away from where I live, a new resort called the Colony just opened last month. There, for a small fee, Eric and I will have our very own condominium for the weekend. Inside it has plenty of space, a Jacuzzi, two bedrooms just in case we have company; the refrigerator will be stocked full of food that we prefer. I spent more time last night picking out what food we wanted than planning this event. More importantly, this getaway will be packed full of peace of quiet. I'm desperately trying to get away from the hustle of everyday life. I quickly dialed Eric's number.

"Hello?" he answered.

"Hello, Mr. Dickerson." I greeted him with a seductive tone of my voice.

"Izzy, I've been trying to call you all day. Where have you been?"

"My cell phone was low battery. I was out running errands. What's going on? Are the kids all right?"

"Baby, they're fine. We need to talk. It doesn't look good for me. I'm coming over," he stated and hung up the phone. I was pacing the floor, looking out the window for every second it took for him to show up in my driveway. Usually, I can sense when something is wrong before it happens. This is throwing me for a loop. Deep down, I didn't have a good feeling and my stomach began to turn, filled with worry and uncertainty.

"What's going on?" I said as he put the truck into park.

"She's really trying to get me. Mirna is playing real nasty." Eric stepped in the house and halfway into the foyer.

"What do you mean? Talk to me," I insisted.

"I'm so pissed right now," he shouted, clutching his fingers together, pacing the floor back and forth.

"Eric, tell me what's going on? What has Mirna done now? Is she threatening to take the kids away?" It's the only thought to get him this angry. Matter of fact, I've never seen this man so mad throughout our whole relationship.

"No, it's not the kids, exactly. Besides, Mirna isn't that crazy to pull a stunt like that. Last year, around May, when we came to terms with the separation agreement, one of the terms stated is that neither one of us could bring the children around the significant other. At the same time when I signed the documentation, I didn't think I would ever find love again. I completely forgot about *that* one small part. This was before I even laid eyes on you. Now, she's trying to hold me up to that. The only time she saw me with you that I know of was the incident at the car dealership. For a while, she hired a private investigator. Today, earlier this morning, she showed me pictures of you, myself, and the kids going to the park, the carnival, mall, and Mount Trashmore, just to name a few. With this bogus leverage that she has above my head, Mirna may be able to take my business away from me. I went to see my lawyer. Most of the day, he was held in court so I went down to the courthouse and waited patiently just to see him. Yes, he said these pictures were very damaging. Izzy, I can't lose my business."

"You can make another business. I will help you."

"I can't let you do that. From the bottom of my heart, I appreciate it, but I'm a man and I wouldn't feel right taking handouts from you, the woman who I truly love."

"I don't mind. I hate to see you like this. Eric, I want you to be happy. What can I do?"

"I want to be happy too but I've worked too hard building up that business to where it is now. If Mirna does get it, she could reap about two hundred thousand dollars, right now from all of my hard work and sacrifice. Most of my clientele and the workers have been with me for years. People don't like change. Izzy, I have to fight for my business. I owe it that much. Mirna is sitting around with nothing else better to do than play with other people's lives. If she gets the business and sells it to the highest bidder, those guys aren't guaranteed a job. Little does she realize, my workers have rents and mortgages to pay every month and mouths to feed."

"How can you fight this? Can you contest the separation agreement?"

"No, my lawyer advised me the only way I could get out of it was to reconcile with Mirna."

"You mean get back together with her?" I asked, taking a deep breath.

"Yes and no. Reconcile means I'm going to have to move back in the house with her and the kids. Once I start living there, it looks to the court of law that we have reconciled. My lawyer said I need to stay for about a month or so. Plus, I need the number to your girlfriend's husband who works at Enterprise rental car center. I'm taking the kids and her to Disney World, which will make me look even better. If the plan goes well, he advised me to lay low with you as well. We can't go out as much in public and seeing the kids is off-limits until the divorce is final. I know it's going to be hard at first but we can get through this," he explained, pulling me closer. I quickly backed away from him.

"You got the damn nerve to ask me for a hookup on a car so you can take her to Disney World? Are you crazy? Have you got no class, Eric? Plus, how do I know you won't get horny one night and slide your dick into her? You just dropped a bomb on me."

"That's not all, she's going to subpoena you, your coworkers, my own momma, sisters, brothers, my workers, and anyone else she can think of."

"Why?" I asked, pissed more than him.

"To ask each and every one person if they saw you with me and the kids. She wants to humiliate me in court."

"I can't let her do that to you or my family. I refuse to let Mirna make a mockery of my business and my life.

"This is too much for me to handle," I conveyed, shaking my head and taking a seat on the couch.

"Izzy, you know where my heart is. Mirna and I have been over long before you even came in the picture. It's as if she's doing this because she doesn't want me, but Mirna doesn't want any other woman to have me, either," he proclaimed resting his left hand gently on top of my heart. I hit his hand away.

"That hurt," Eric stated.

"Money isn't everything. In time, I hope you see that. I do understand and know how hard you worked for your business. You've pretty much made up your mind. I'm not going to participate in this game any longer. Besides, you're still her husband and you let her do whatever the hell she wants." *Not knowing what those two are doing in that house would drive me crazy,* I thought.

"We can do this. I'll call you and see you when I can. Once I'm back at the house, I know Mirna will be looking through the phone so I'm going to get another cell phone. No more than three months do we have to endure this," he explained, looking right into my eyes.

"Shut up and get the hell out of my house. It kills me how you would even think I'm going to let you call me from another cell phone. I can't hardly see you at all and if we do, you and I pretty much have to sneak around. I'm not doing that. I love you but I'm not lowering my standards of having a relationship. If you were a real man, you would have let me make my own choice. You come in the house demanding me to be part of the team and your conniving plan. I don't have to put up with this. Eric, you have too much drama. Go find your own rental hookup. I can find someone else who doesn't have so many problems. What do we got together, Eric? I thought it was love, but your love for money is far more important than me. Don't try to use your family and me as alternative scapegoats as why you're going back to live with Mirna. Say what is loud and proud. *Money!* If that's pretty much all you care about why should I stay with you? Why should I continue to love you? My good pussy can be going to another man. The way I look at, I'm better off cutting my losses, before I get even deeper with you. Lose my number. You don't exist to me any-more," I announced, opening the door for him to leave.

Once right outside, Eric turned around.

"Izzy, please . . ." Before I heard any more garbage

coming from his mouth, I kindly slammed the door in his face.

It wasn't easy calling and canceling the reservations at the Colony Resort. I was looking forward to getting away. I refused to shred one tear for Eric Dickerson. Within the next two hours, I called Vera to come over to the house to help me change the locks. After calling three times, she didn't pick up so I took measures in my own hands. I made a mental note to buy the book *Handy Work For Dummies* at Home Depot. One thing is for sure, I had to have the locks changed at the house, tonight. It was after-hours so I was forced to pay double. Most likely, the guy who came to the house was lying just to make an extra dollar but I didn't care. Eric did have a key to my house and I had a key to his home. I will put his in the mail tomorrow. I didn't want him to give him any reason to contact me. After locking up the house for the night and walking upstairs to my bathroom, I went to search through the medicine cabinet for my sedatives. It was going to be the only way I was going to get some sleep, tonight.

Friday morning quickly came and I had twenty voice mails on the house phone, forty-seven messages on my cell phones, and ten text messages. I didn't even bother to listen to any of the voice mails. The text messages were instantly erased. What I did intend to this day was to make a call to Verizon customer service and change all of my numbers. The work number wasn't getting changed but it would be an easy fix because I just wouldn't answer the phone. My main objective today was go to the bank and inquire about borrowing money to start up another business. Pondering whether I would decide on Tropical Smoothie Café, Quiznos subs or Cold Stone Creamery. All three were places that I frequently went to. I'm sure I wasn't the only one.

One Week Later

I phoned all my friends and family and gave strict instructions not to give my number to anyone. I hadn't been in the coffee shop for seven whole days. For all the team knew, I was still on vacation. Once I go back, I'm going to try my best to hold back the tears, if someone asks, "how was the new resort with Eric?" Seven days and counting and I haven't shed one tear. I was so proud of myself that I went and bought a small round strawberry passion ice cream cake from Cold Stone Creamery. It consisted of a buttery graham cracker crust and a base stacked strawberry cake and ice cream, literally. On top, there lay sweet strawberries.

The bank had no problem in lending me the start-up money for the business. I talked to Jimmy about it, as well. He said if I borrowed from him, not a penny of interest would be charged. The previous money I borrowed from his was all paid back. My word of mouth and creditability goes along way with Mr. Risoto.

Finally, a decision had to be made about which restaurant I wanted to start up. I chose the Tropical Smoothie Café. The location would be in downtown Suffolk on Main Street, where there is a lot of traffic. Besides, there were already a Quiznos sub and Cold Stone Creamery on the street. The location of the business is just as vital as the product you're selling. A store developer assigned to this area scheduled an appointment to personally meet me and explained their policies and procedures. With my signature on the dotted line, I was again a proud owner of yet another franchise called Tropical Smoothie Café. This new venture was going to help me prosper and become even more successful. Plus, it would keep me busy and my mind off of Eric Dickerson.

Chapter 51

The days I did work at Starbucks were always in the mornings. Eric called the coffee shop relentlessly. I instructed all of my team members to kill him with kindness and say the same thing over and over again. He would say, "May I speak to Izzy Preston?" Their response would be, "She's not here. Would you like a cup of coffee?" Next, he would say, "do you know when she will be back?" Their response would be in the same tone as before, "She's not here. Would you like a cup of coffee?" This would irritate him to the fullest, yet he still kept calling. I even switched the cars I drove from the Escalade to the Lexus truck. Soon after, Eric got smart and started coming in the mornings, but at the same time. As we got ready in the morning to set the coffee shop, we got ready in the morning to hide me from Eric. When someone spotted him out of the window, I would run to the back. If I couldn't get there in time, I would hide under the counter where I wouldn't be seen. He's been coming in for the last three months, desperately wanting to talk to me. The first two months were very hard on me.

I tried hard not to shed one tear, but either my willpower or broken heart gave in. For about a month, I cried so much, my eyes were red and swollen. Eric broke my heart but time will restore it, someday. Now, I wonder if my heart can even love someone again. Finally, a week ago, Eric has stopped coming in here. I hope the daily charades are over.

Six weeks ago, I was forced to change my number *again* because he went to his sister's house and snuck to get her cell phone to look up my *new* phone number. It costs fifteen dollars to change my number and I was furious because I wasn't willing to spend any more time and energy wasted on someone who I feel just cared about money. Maybe I was meant to have a relationship to establish an endless friendship with his sister. She promised to tell him nothing going on with me. Vickie has been neutral in the situation. Right is right and wrong is wrong. Even though Eric is her baby brother, she admitted that my choice to end the relationship was a fair one. My coworkers felt both of us were still in love with each other because of the lengths I go to avoid him and the lengths he goes to try to get a small glimpse of me or hear my voice on the phone for only a few moments.

Tropical Smoothie Café is making a profit of seventeen thousand a month and counting. At first, I thought I wouldn't be able to swing nineteen hundred a month, but it's doable. Hopefully, the rent will not increase when the lease is expired. I hired a manager and five other people to work the store. I may go to work once or twice a week. These employees are given opportunities to the same benefits as far as health insurance, dental, and vision insurance is concerned. Not to mention the 401(k) plan is offered as well.

Today was employee appreciation day for the employees, of course, and their families. After reserving seven picnic tables at Mount Trashmore in Virginia Beach, I ordered a clown and pony rides for the children. Seeing a clown blow up balloons and turn them into giraffes, lions, tigers, cars, flowers, and anything else a child can request would spark their interest. Also, the clown will offer face painting. The pony rides will be fifteen minutes apiece. Next to the picnic tables are a tennis court and a basketball court. Not to mention, I rented a cotton candy machine. It will make strawberry, grape, and blueberry cotton candy. Last but not least, the kids will be able to make their own snow cones, getting to choose from over two hundred flavors. Traditional flavors shall be selected such as piña colada, kiwi lime, black cherry, peach, apple, raspberry, orange, cherry, grape, passion fruit, lime, watermelon, bubble gum, tangerine, and coconut. The company, Snow Cone Caravan, will be offering new flavors such as papaya, cinnamon, birthday cake, cappuccino, plum, candy apple, caramel, peppermint, eggnog custard, margarita, peanut butter, white chocolate and chips, coffee, and licorice.

Pollard's Chicken will be catering fried chicken, fried fish, coleslaw, baked beans, ham sandwiches, fruit tray, vegetable tray, and scallops wrapped with bacon. In addition, the company Pork Heaven will be offering BBQ sandwiches. As an added bonus, they will be working the grills for me placing hot dogs, hamburgers, barbecue chicken, and steaks on it.

Chapter 52

Vera had been a real trouper in helping get me through the long nights without Eric. Now, he doesn't even come up in our conversation anymore. Still, I couldn't but wonder if I deserved a broken heart along with the hurt and pain because of all the messing around I did with married and taken men. Was karma finally changing up with me? If so, how long would the wrath last? What could I do to redeem myself?

We're on our way to Smokey Bones to have a taste of Southern-style ribs. What I enjoy most is the cornbread.

"Guess who Bernard saw?" Vera stated after the waitress seated us at the booth.

"Who?" I had no idea who she was talking about.

"Guess?"

"I don't know."

"He saw Alicia at the Norfolk courthouse. She was tried for attempting to steal a flat-screen television at Kmart."

"How many inches was it?" I inquired.

"I'm not sure. Bernard might have said thirty inches."

"Hmm, anything over the cost of five hundred dollars is grand larceny. Right?"

"I guess. Bernard knows better than we would," Vera insisted.

"What sentence did she get?" I inquired and stopped looking at the menu. "Well, she got off on probation. Bernard said once she left the courtroom she was going to anyone who would listen to her sob story about how she can't feed her kids and was asking them for a dollar," she explained, shaking her head.

"Alicia doesn't have any kids."

"She doesn't have any that we know of. You know she was probably lying to get high yet another time."

"Vera, now that's a shame. At times, I look back and reminisce about our summer camp days and never once did I think our friendship would turn out like this. You and I are the only ones left standing."

"I still talk to Rachel and Alicia. We're not as close as we were but I still make it a point to call them on holidays, birthdays, and check up on them from time to time."

"You know I haven't talked either one of them in a while," I assured her.

"Izzy, if you can forgive your parents for everything they've done, you can forgive Alicia and Rachel."

"Hmm, mmm. It's easy for you to say. Alicia didn't waste a thousand of your dollars."

"You had to be angry, but for how long? Don't waste your energy dwelling on the past. You take holding grudges to a new level. Let it go. What is the use in you being so angry and bitter?"

"I'm not pissed off anymore. Alicia used me and I thought despite her being hooked on heroin, she would still treat me a friend. Rachel is too judgemental and needs to get off her snobby high horse."

"Don't hold her actions so much against her. Alicia getting high off of heroin and doing anything to achieve that goal is not the girl that we know and grew up with. Rachel still feels terrible about the way she treated you. She has realized you were a true friend to her. Again, call Alicia and Rachel to check up on them. Will you at least think about it?"

"Maybe," I hinted.

"I'm not suggesting you welcome them back with open arms but you could pick up the phone and call to see how they're doing."

"Is Rachel's cell phone number still the same?" I asked, pulling out mine to insert her number in my phone contacts.

"Yes, it is."

"I'm surprised Alicia has a cell phone. Maybe you're right. I'll give Rachel a call when I get home but certainly not Alicia. I have to admit, I do miss my godson."

"Alicia is back over at the women's shelter but on strict probation. If she is arrested one more time, then she will get kicked out."

"How many times did she go to jail?" I asked out of curiosity.

"The ones I know are about fifteen times."

"What has she gone for?"

"Do you really want to know?"

"Yeah."

"Stealing and prostitution."

"Whoa."

"Hello, ladies. My name is Destiny and I'm going to be your waiter this evening. How are you two doing tonight?" she asked.

"Fine," we responded in unison.

"Can I start you off with some drinks tonight?"

"I'll have an apple martini," Vera preferred.

"I'll have a sweet tea with two pieces of lemon," I stated.

"I'll be right back with your drinks. Are you ready to order or do you need more time?"

"We need more time," I replied. Vera and I were so busy talking we didn't have much time to look in the menu.

"Here are your drinks," she announced while placing them on the table. "Now, are you ready to order or you still need a few minutes?"

"We'll have the spinach artichoke dip with extra feta cheese and two orders of the baby back ribs," I replied after taking a sip of the sweet tea. The baby back ribs were tender, sweet, and succulent with the BBQ sauce. The meat would literally fall off the bone.

"What are your sides?"

"Steamed broccoli and a baked potato for me," Vera stated.

"I want French fries and steamed broccoli," I replied.

"I'm going to put in your order. The appetizer will be out before your entrées," she explained and walked away.

"I'm going to use the restroom. Watch my purse," Vera stated.

"All right," I responded. My cell phone was ringing but I didn't answer phone numbers I wasn't able to recognize just in case it was Eric. If the person wanted to speak to me that bad, he or she will leave a message.

"Isabel, you will never guess who I saw coming from the bathroom."

"Who?" I asked. I wish Vera would just spit it out instead of playing games.

"Brian Drexler."

"What? Really? Where is he?"

"Brian is coming this way after he uses the bathroom. You know he had a thing for you all throughout high school." All through out middle school and high school, Brian and I had a close bond. After we graduated, we drifted apart because he went off to North Carolina A&T and I was too busy for any and everybody dealing with Bruce. He would have choked me if another man called the house or my cell phone. I was simply looking for love in all the wrong places. Now, I've learned to realize that a man shouldn't fill the void of my father. A man should be my companion. Looking back, I still wish I would have beat his ass even more. Since the police took their sweet time taking Bruce to the hospital the day he was arrested, he is only legally blind in his left eye. It gives me comfort to know that he suffered like he made me suffer. At night, I woke up in cold sweats dreaming about him kicking me in the stomach over and over again. Maybe I should go to counseling. The cost isn't a worry. Besides, my health insurance covers 100 percent of the visits.

"Now, I know. Why didn't you tell me?"

"Girl, he swore me to secrecy. Plus, you haven't gotten any in a while."

"So what? I may think he looks ugly."

"No, you won't," she insisted, watching for him to come this way.

"If you were sworn to secrecy back in high school, why are you spilling the beans now?"

"This isn't high school days any more. Besides, we graduated over fifteen years ago, Izzy. Here he comes."

"Hey, Isabel Preston."

"Hi Brian," I greeted him with a hug. Brian heavily favored the R&B singer Tyrese, including those pearly-white teeth and a chiseled chest.

"What are you ladies doing here?"

"About to pig out," Vera stated.

"My boys are at the bar having a few drinks and watching the game."

"Sit down," Vera insisted. He sat by me.

"So what's been going on with you for the last fifteen years?" I asked.

"I got married and have a daughter."

"How old is she?" I questioned.

"Katlyn is six going on twenty-four." We all started laughing.

"My wife—excuse me, ex-wife—got divorced two years ago."

"What happened?"

"Sorry to say, but our marriage ended up as a statistic. What's the number-one reason people get divorced?"

"Getting married for the wrong reasons?" I mentioned, hoping Brian wouldn't playing guessing games tonight as well.

"Money," Vera blurted out.

"You're absolutely right. Bethany racked up sixty thousand in credit card debt."

"Whoa—and you didn't know?" I questioned.

"Ya'll women know how you do. You can be very sneaky and conniving when you want to be."

"So I assume the credit card bills weren't forwarded to your address?" Vera inquired.

"Of course not. She had them going to a post-office box down the street from the house. Bethany wanted the finer things in life and simply couldn't afford it. I wanted her to start up a retirement plan. She wanted a four-thousand-dollar purse. I couldn't even tell you the name of it. That's not all, she took out a second mortgage on the house for one hundred thousand dollars and paid off the sixty-thousand credit card debt. Then, she maxed out the cards again. Her plan crumbled before her face when she missed a payment," he replied, shaking his head.

"How did she take a second mortgage on the home without your name?"

"She forced my name. The loan officer was her cousin. Bethany told him I couldn't make it because I was working."

"Wow, what a story," I confessed, taking a deep breath, hoping the person I marry won't do me like that.

"Once we sold the house, most of her half of the house proceeds went to paying off credit card bills. Keeping up the Joneses isn't worth it."

"Ladies, here are your entrées and the appetizer. The cooks failed to prepare it before your food came out. I talked with the manager and he's going to give you the appetizer for free. I apologize for the error."

"It's all right. Thank you," Vera responded, feasting her eyes on her plate.

"Is there anything else you may need? Can I bring you some ketchup, vinegar, hot sauce or more BBQ sauce?"

"Can I have a Long Island iced-tea?"

"May I see your driver's license?"

"Sure." I was loving the fact the waiter thought I looked to be under the age of twenty-one. Those days are long gone.

"And for you?"

"No, I'm good. Thank you," Vera replied before tearing into a rib.

"Miss, may I have Hennessy?"

"Sure, I'll be right back with your drinks."

"Brian, do you want some ribs?" I asked.

"Nah, I'm stuffed. I just finished eating them. They were excellent, tonight."

"Did you still pursue your dream of being an accountant?"

"Yes, I sure did. I work for Avantais, a major accounting company that does heavy-duty bookkeeping for many leading companies in this country.

"What about you, Izzy?"

"I own a Starbucks in Virginia Beach and a Tropical Smoothie Café in Suffolk."

"I bet you have your hands full."

"No, not really. My motto is to take each day one day at a time. I can't be in two places at once. Besides, I have the best employees who believe in teamwork to get the job done."

"And you, Vera?"

"I work for a health insurance company that processes claims. I'm one of the bigwigs over there but I don't let it go to my head," she explained, running her fingers through her hair.

For the next two hours, Vera, Brian, and I reminisced about the past and talked about our plans for the future. Four Hennessys for Brian and two more Long Island iced-teas for me, we were a little tipsy. Brian and I could hold our liquor. He was kind enough to pay for the meal and the drinks.

"Brian, it was so nice seeing you. Please keep in touch. It's getting late and I don't want my husband blowing up my cell phone," Vera explained.

" 'Bye, Vera. I will call you later," I explained as she was putting her coat on. "Don't worry, I'll be all right to drive."

"If you get pulled over by the police for your blood-alcohol level being way too high, please don't call me," she joked.

"We'll be fine," Brian assured her.

" 'Bye," she waved and walked toward the front door.

"Izzy, do you want to go to my place so we can keep talking? The employees are starting to give us dirty looks because the restaurant will be closing in fifteen minutes," he suggested, looking down at his watch.

"Where do you live?"

"I live down the street in the Baywell Manor apartments, a gated community."

"I'll follow you, Please drive slow, I'm getting sleepy," I responded before drink the last bit of my drink.

"Here, let me help you with your coat," he announced, picking it up for me. *What a gentleman*, I thought.

Once we got outside, I felt as though someone was watching me. It's a very creepy feeling. The hairs on my arms started sticking up and my heart was beating rapidly. Still, I stayed late some nights at the coffee shop by myself. For some added protection, I carried my .22 caliber pistol. I forgot to take it out of my purse the night before. I've haven't drank this much alcohol since the night of prom, I thought while buckling my seat belt.

"You have a nice home," I announced, looking around his two-bedroom apartment. His daughter's room was decorated in the Disney Channel's cartoon show, *The Proud Family*. She had the comforter, sheets, blankets, pillowcases, lamp, telephone, rug, television, and desk to do homework on. Courtesy of Lauren, I knew about *The Proud Family*. We watch those shows whenever Lauren comes over to the house. With the rest of the apartment, it depicted an Asian furniture decor.

"Thank you. I hired an interior decorator." I started to giggle.

"What's so funny? Do I have something in my hair or on my shirt?" Brian inquired, rubbing his fingers through his hair and looking throughout his body.

"Me too," I admitted.

"You hired one too? I thought you women were all the same, loving to shop and decorate any and everything."

"No, not Izzy Preston. I'm not interested in interior design in the least bit. I shot a few ideas to Ms. Poole and she made it come alive. Plus, she quoted me low rates."

"It seems as if you got what you wanted."

"I sure did. If I was to take on the task, it would have never got done," I assured him, shaking my head.

" Izzy, where are my manners? Please, have a seat. What do you do in your spare time?" Brian asked as we sat down on the couch.

"Well, let me see. In my spare time, I go pick up Lauren and we have so much fun. A few times, I brought her to work with me just for an hour."

"You must get Little Miss Lauren in the job field early."

"The earlier it is, the better it will be. She's my future and will probably be taking care of me when I get old."

"How much do you pay her?"

"She doesn't get paid in money like you and I do. Lauren gets payed in Teddy Graham Crackers. If she's worked a hard day, I'll give her an Oreo." We both laughed.

"Is there anything else you do?"

"Yes, I volunteer at two shelters. One is for battered women and the other for pregnant teens. Yvette, the director, has been an inspiration to those women. I donate my time answering calls on the twenty-four-hour hotline. We get a lot of calls during the day and really late at night. These times are when the boyfriends and husbands are not around so the women can talk without so much looking over their shoulder. The youngest girl I've seen pregnant was twelve years old. Her stepfather was molesting her. The sad thing about is that her mother thought she was lying at first. Then, once reality set in her daughter was pregnant with her husband's baby, the mother accused the daughter of seducing the stepfather."

"Wow, that is a terrible story," he responded, almost in disbelief.

"The baby ended up being adopted. After the DNA test proved he was the father, he was sentenced to fifteen years in prison. The young woman was adopted by a loving family. The situation did turn out for the best. What irked the crap out of me was the mother. It was if she was brainwashed by her husband. If my husband raped my daughter, death would be too good for him."

"What would you do?"

"You mean what haven't I done to the nasty culprit. First, he would get tied up and beaten with a scorching hot iron. Next, I would cut off the penis in little chunks, which caused so much trouble. Finally, I would sow up his butthole and keep feeding him refried beans over and over again. Pain and constant agony would be the best solution for him for taking away a child's innocence forever."

"Izzy, you have a vivid imagination."

"What do you do in your leisure time?"

"I like to play ball and participate in the Big Brothers program. I like to mentor to the boys I get."

"How many have you had so far?"

"Two."

"You are making a huge difference in a young man's life."

"Thanks and believe me when I tell you, Izzy, it's a great feeling. I love to give back."

Brian and I talked for at least another hour. Next, he offered me the remote control and I gladly took it, tuning into old episodes of the HBO show *Sex and the City*. In this episode, Miranda's son was being christened. Too tired and tipsy to drive home, Brian offered me his bed and he would take the couch or the twin-size bed in his daughter's room.

"Do you have a spare comb and brush? I accidentally left mine at home lying on the bathroom counter," I inquired, rubbing my fingers through my hair. Usually, I never forget my comb and brush. If I don't comb my hair and wrap it around my head, it will look like a bush in the morning with kinks I won't have the energy to deal with.

"Yes, I sure do. I'll be right back with a T-shirt and pajama pants and the other essentials that you need. I must warn you the clothes will be a little too big for you."

"Okay, that's fine. Anything is better than nothing." I bet Brian would like to see me with nothing on as well. All his attention was on me, tonight. I never noticed this kind of behavior before.

"Here you are. A spare toothbrush is in the medicine cabinet," he stated, handing me everything.

"Thanks, I'll go change in the bathroom." While in the bathroom, I sent Vera a text message telling her I was alive and where exactly I was and who I was with. Usually, she would text message me back within five minutes. Since Vera didn't, I knew she was knocked out in her bed.

"I'm mostly all done and ready to go to sleep. I just need to comb my hair," I announced, coming back into the living room with the clothes I wore to the restaurant in my arms.

"Come here and let me do it," he insisted, taking the comb out of my hand. Brian took control back over the remote and turned the channel to BET with a show that played R&B songs. Singer Joe's video, "All The Things," was playing now. I didn't put that much up of a fight because I loved when someone else combed my hair. I kneeled down on the brown carpet floor while Brian sat on the front of the couch. It felt so relaxing when Brian was combing my hair, almost where I was feeling more and more sleepy and sensitive to his touch. After thirty minutes of pure bliss, Brian stopped combing my hair and started rubbing my shoulders all the way down to my fingers. My head was in his lap. Brian gently kissed me on the lips. His lips were moist and ever so soft.

"Let me make love to you, tonight. I've been dreaming about this night for more than twenty years."

"Why didn't you say anything?"

"I was scared, nervous, and didn't want to run the risk of getting rejected by you," he explained while taking off my ocean blue boy shorts.

"We'll never know what could have happened."

"Yeah, you're right so let's make up for lost time and start making our own precious memories," he proclaimed. Brian started rubbing on my breasts. I wasn't finished with his lips, yet. I motioned his lips to meet mine again. He kneeled down on the carpet floor and started rubbing and then gently biting my breasts through his T-shirt I was wearing. It instantly got me wet. Brian didn't have to do it for me. I took off my shirt and he picked me off the floor and carried me into the bedroom and sat me on the bed. He started sucking on my breasts, my neck, my ears, and toes. I closed my eyes and enjoyed him exploring my body.

"I bet your pussy taste sweet," he insisted while taking his clothes off and putting on a condom.

"Get a taste and see, I'm only making a suggestion," I shared with him, looking right into his eyes, only taking a quick glance at his dick. Nice size, I thought.

Brian licked the bottom of my pussy and slowly to the top. This was making me even more wet. The foreplay he was dishing out was literally going to make me come. Next, he started massaging my clitoris in a circular motion. After I came, I was so grateful to have gotten lucky with a guy who knew what he was doing down there.

Brian turned me over on my stomach. He then lay on top of me and entered his seven inches into my ripe pink pussy. This is what I called doggystyle with the deepest strokes. I could tell Brian was trying his best to show me what he was working with. Our hands tightly clutched together.

"Izzy, I love you so much and have for a long time. Neither of us are with anyone, give me a chance," he whispered in my ear after giving me yet another deep stroke.

He came and both of us were drenched in sweat. *Damn, that was good,* I thought. After changing the sheets, Brian and I took a hot shower together, knowing it would help me sleep better.

"Let's talk about this in the morning. Both of us are too drunk to think clearly right now," I suggested to him in a soft-toned voice. Deep down, I didn't feel the same about him. Maybe in time, I would.

"All right," he agreed and kissed me on the lips before drifting off to sleep.

The clock read 3:10 in the morning. I had the worst headache and got up from out the bed to search in my purse in the living room for some kind of relief. Tylenols, here I come, I thought, anticipating getting back into the bed. Rummaging through my purse, I hoped to find them.

"You really just wrote me off like a bad check, Izzy. You hurt me deep down in my heart," a voice confessed, pointing to the chest area of their body.

"What are you doing here? How did you get in here?" I asked, scared to death. My heart started beating fast. The hairs on my arms were standing up.

"It took some cooperation but the security guard at the front post gave me the key to this apartment after I shot him in the eye," Bruce explained after licking his double barrel shotgun. I can't believe I was in love with a violent maniac.

"No number to contact you and no visits."

"Bruce, what are you doing out of prison?"

"I got out on a technicality. The police didn't thoroughly do their job," he explained while picking up my light purple V-neck sweater and dark purple skirt and smelling it. The Greensville Correctional Center was supposed to notify me if his sentence time had changed.

"You still smell the same."

"When did you get out?"

"About three months ago and I've been watching you ever since. Now, I've finally caught you with your boyfriend," he laughed in a devilish tone.

"Get out," I demanded.

"I heard you two in the bedroom fucking, but nobody can lay it down like me. Isn't that right, Isabel?"

"I'm warning you to leave me alone," I demanded, tightly clutching my purse.

"Don't think I don't know about our daughter. Where is she?"

"What are you talking about?" I questioned, literally shaking.

"Listen, Izzy, before you ask, it's a small world out there. One of the ladies that worked at the pregnancy shelter, her son happened to share a cell with me. His mother, Carla Lopez, was so moved by your story that she told him. She shared it with him on one of their weekend visits and the rest is history. Where is my daughter, Izzy? I'm not playing no more games with you." *That information was supposed to be strictly confidential,* I thought.

"Get out now, before I call the cops," I yelled back, quietly pushing the 911 buttons on my cell phone. Hopefully, they could hear the conversation and pick up where the location is.

"I'm not going anywhere. Your ass is mine, Izzy. I'm going to enjoy killing you, but first, you're going to tell you where my daughter is. You belong to me and I want to see my little girl, right now. Where is she?" he asked, grabbing my neck, choking me, slamming me up against the wall. I started losing consciousness when Opal appeared out of nowhere and suddenly said, "Don't give up. Fight back, Izzy," she proclaimed repeatedly.

I got up enough nerve and strength to take the .22-caliber gun out of my purse.

"What's going on?" Brian asked out of confusion.

"This is none of your concern," Bruce announced and pointed the gun at Brian. Luckily, I shot Bruce one time. He immediately fell to the floor.

"Izzy, it didn't have to go down like this. I love you and I just wanted to see my daughter, Sophia. Years ago, I denied being the father because I was too scared and selfish to bring a newborn into this world," Bruce confessed on the carpet floor, covered in his own blood. When he reached to grab my leg, I stomped the hell out of his neck. His shouts of pain were joy to my ears. The police banged on the door. I fell to the door. The room went black.

I fainted on to the carpet floor. After waking up after thirty minutes and thoroughly checked by the paramedics, I felt all right to get up. The paramedic had said that my body went into shock. Plus, I had a swollen neck from Bruce squeezing me. By this time, Vera and Bernard were here. The police assured us that I would not be indicted for murder. The police officer ruled it as self-defense especially since I had dialed 911 and it recorded most of the conversation I had with Bruce before the shots were fired. Thank God I had a concealed-weapons permit. Many years ago, I tossed the caliber Bruce gave to me because I knew it was hot and purchased my very own. It turns out Bruce not only killed the security guard but also the social worker, Carla Lopez, at the women's shelter. A witness saw them arguing because he wanted to know who had Sophia and where was she.

Vera and Bernard must have brought Brian up to speed on my relationship with Bruce. He was so understanding, empathetic, and felt guilty because he didn't get in time to help before Bruce put his hands on me.

"Brian, I'm so sorry that I brought my drama to your door. Your carpet floor looks terrible. I'm so grateful nothing happened in your daughter's bedroom. Please send me the bill for your carpet getting cleaned. It's the least I can do," I explained with my voice weak and hoarse. I didn't want to speak too much.

"Izzy, don't worry about the carpet. It can be replaced. I'm going to start cleaning up. Please, just worry about feeling better and getting your strength back. It took a lot of courage to stand up to your violent ex-boyfriend."

"Thank you," I replied while giving him a short-lived hug. My body was so sore, head to toe.

"Call me if you need anything," he strongly suggested.

"I will," I assured him with tears of relief in my eyes. Never again, would I have to worry about Bruce Tripson hurting me or Sophia.

I had to go down to the police station to answer a few questions and then I was free to go. Ending up staying and sleeping at Vera's house wasn't a bad idea for the next couple of days. The following day, Vera took me to the primary-care physician to get examined just in case the paramedics had missed anything. My neck was swollen, appearing as a more of a purplish color. Dr.

Munden ruled out any broken bones or serious injuries. He said the bruising and swelling would go away in time. Dr. Munden prescribed a medication called Xanax to help with panic and anxiety attacks and Motrin eight-hundred milligrams for the pain. Dr. Munden wanted to cover all his bases especially if I suffered a panic attack.

It was a cold and rainy day on Carla Lopez's funeral. Brian came with me. Her thirteen-year-old daughter, Nina, cried out for losing yet another family member. Her father died in an automobile accident seven years ago, her brother was sentenced to ten years in prison for the participation in an armed robbery, and now her mother was gone forever. Before leaving, I didn't hesitate to tell Carla's mother to call me if she needed anything. Bruce should be rotting in hell, right now, for all the lives he's destroyed.

Three Weeks Later

My parents and Grandma Elaine found out about Bruce dying by hands. All I revealed is I'm all right and no one else was hurt. Avoiding them was starting to worry my grandmother with her relentless voice mails. I was on my way over to her house to talk with her.

"Hey," I called out to find all three of them sitting in the living room. Lauren was asleep in her playpen.

"Hi, Isabel, we need to talk."

"About what?" I asked, rummaging through my purse for a piece of bubble gum. I needed something to calm my nerves because they all were going to want to take a stroll down memory lane.

"Bruce Tripson. It's been over all the news. Now, come

on in here and sit down," Grandma directed, pointing to the couch. I took a seat next to Daddy.

"We're all worried about you. A month ago, you killed a man who you loved very much some time ago. We just want to know, why? What happened? Why did you two break up in the first place? Why was he looking for you after he got out of jail?"

"He wasn't the nicest boyfriend, after all. In front of you all, he was a complete gentleman. Don't get me wrong, things weren't bad at the time; however, Bruce could get violent. He hit me a lot and I couldn't take it anymore."

"Why didn't you say anything?" Mom and Daddy asked in unison.

"Mom, I didn't want to worry you about me. Besides, I knew you were worried enough. Anger, resentment, and pain wouldn't allow me to share it with you. Still now, I don't want to talk about it. He's dead, now I can move on with my life."

"How did he know you were with Brian at his apartment?" Grandma inquired.

"Bruce saw me leaving the restaurant with him and driving to his apartment."

"Where did he hit you?"

"Everywhere," I replied, not wanting to go into explicit detail.

"Isabel Preston, as feisty as you were growing up in this house, please tell me you hit him back at least time."

"More than once," I said, smiling.

"Good," she responded with a sigh of relief.

"We want to make sure you're all right," Grandma insisted.

"I'm all right, Grandma, but I do have something to tell each of you," I announced.

"I gave birth to a daughter named Sophia," I explained,

pulling out pictures of her in my purse. My favorite picture of her is three months, dressed up as an angel.

"Girl, no wonder I didn't' see you for ten months," Grandma reminisced.

"Where is she?"

"She is with her adoptive parents. At the time, I thought it was the best decision. Bruce was sentenced to prison for many years and I truly wasn't ready to be a mother and didn't want Sophia to suffer for it."

"Isabel Preston, you sure know how to make my heart race. Bruce was abusive and now there's a baby. Please, in the future, if you need to talk or need anything, please come to us. You're my daughter, I love you dearly, and there's nothing I wouldn't do for you. I'm so sorry we lost so many years of it," Mom explained, hugging me.

"I love you too Mom."

"We can move forward and put the past behind us," Dad proclaimed, picking up Lauren, who was waking up from a nap.

"I got news for you, Izzy," Mom explained.

"What? You're buying me the custom-made cotton candy machine I've been wanting since I was nine years old."

"Ah, no, if you can take the time off, we want the whole family to go to Jamaica."

"Grandma too?"

"Yes, she will be coming as well. We haven't gone in so long."

"Everyone would love to see you and Lauren," Daddy added.

"Yeah, they would, but don't get it twisted. Everyone wants to see the new edition to the family even more. Once Lauren was born, I lost my crown of being spoiled," I teased.

Chapter 53

"Hey Izzy," Brian greeted me as I walked in to the door.

"Hi," I replied, feeling awkward about walking in to the same apartment where I killed Bruce. Ever since that night, the nightmares have stopped. I'm truly at peace with the situation.

"How have you been feeling?"

"I got my strength back."

"Glad to hear. I notice your neck isn't bruised anymore," he responded, gently caressing it.

"Yeah, I'm good as new," I proclaimed, motioning to sit on the couch, noticing the whole carpet had been replaced.

"What else has been going on?"

"Today in the mail, I received a brand-new school picture of Sophia. I forgot to bring it over here with me," I explained, smiling.

"I'm sure she's just as beautiful as her mother. How was the trip?"

"If I could put it into one word, it was wonderful. I

needed it after everything that has happened. We had plenty of fun in the sun. I read about three books while sipping on piña coladas. Lauren and I ate many ices and made sand castles. She didn't particularly like the water especially when it splashed in her face. Daddy's side of the family was fighting just to hold her. Enough about me, how are you doing? You've been through a lot too. Plus, no matter what you say, I will always feel guilty for what Bruce did. What if your daughter was here? What if you were really hurt? Again, I know I sound like a broken record, but from the bottom of my heart, I'm truly sorry for what happened that night."

"Izzy, first of all, Katlyn is doing fine. Earlier, I took her to Kangaroo Jack, a fun haven for kids. She had a ball," he laughed.

"I'll have to tell my parents about the place. Lauren is full of energy and loves to run around."

"Please, stop apologizing for something that you couldn't control. It happened, so let's not dwell on the past. Yeah, Katlyn could have been over, but she wasn't. I could have been hurt, but I wasn't. You said if there's anything I want from you all I had to do was ask, right?"

"Yeah," I responded, eager to know what he wanted.

"What I want is a future with you, if you let me."

"You threw me for a loop when you said you loved me. I had no idea."

"Yes, my feelings still haven't changed."

"Right now, I'm not ready to be in a relationship with you. Would you be willing to be friends?"

"Anything is better than nothing," he agreed with a half smile. Brian was somewhat disappointed. I was surprised he wanted to be with me after everything that had happened.

"Are you up for a movie?" I asked, while holding the tickets.

"What are you trying to see?"

"*Perfect Stranger* with Halle Berry. I'm a sucker for mysteries."

"Let's go," he replied.

"As long as you let me buy the popcorn, candy, and drinks."

"I'm a nachos man."

"All right, nachos as well," I said, smiling.

"Agreed," he replied, nodding his head.

Chapter 54

Since being broadcasted on the news, Bruce's mother had contacted me begging for money because she didn't have enough to bury him. During the course of our entire relationship, I can count on one hand how many times I saw her. In a way, I blame her for the way he turned out. Violence and abuse are learned behavior. His mother's boyfriend gave her many forceful blows. To this day, she is still with the man, getting beat down.

One of Jimmy Risoto's contacts in this area had told him about the incident. As soon as heard, he called me to check up on me. Jimmy said if he knew what had happened, Bruce would have been handled. I assured him the worst was over and appreciated him calling.

It was a usual busy day at the coffee shop. The crew had stopped walking on eggshells, asking me every other five minutes if I was all right. Customers, especially women, who came inside the building all voiced their opinion. The majority ruling felt I was courageous for sticking up to Bruce. Really, I looked at it as protecting my child. If I had to die for her to be safe and grow up in a loving environment, so be it. Lately, I've been volunteering more of my time at the battered women's shelter. Yvette honored me with a gold medal of bravery to show an example to the women living at the shelter that they didn't have lie down and take the violence.

"Hello, Rachel," I stated as she walked up to the counter.

"Hello, Izzy. I couldn't reach you on the phone so I figured it would be a good idea to come down here and check out your business. I'm proud of you. You've done well for yourself," she explained.

"Thank you. I was going to call you but I got tied up."

"Yeah, I know. I saw what happened on the news. It's terrible what measures you had to go through to get peace from him. Plus, it made me realize, life is too short to hold grudges. I'm sorry what I said that night. At the time, my husband was cheating on me and I took my anger and frustration out on you. It was wrong and I'm sorry."

"I accept your apology."

"Thank you," she replied, giving me a hug from over the counter.

"How's Michael doing?"

"He's getting big. I signed him for football season. He's ready and excited to score some touchdowns on the field."

"Well, I got to see my little man play some time. I do miss him."

"I'll e-mail you all the dates, locations, and times of all his football games."

"Did you want to place an order?"

"Sir, I'll get an iced espresso," she answered, getting out her wallet.

"Don't worry about paying for it. This is on me," I said with a smile.

"Thanks," she replied as I was preparing her drink.

"So, are you a true Starbuckser?" I inquired, trying to start up a conversation and handing her the ice-cold drink.

"I drink it maybe once a week. It's a luxury and I have to spread out my money for indulgences. This isn't the only indulgence I have."

"What else do you like?"

"Hmm, let me see, Krispy Kreme and Dunkin' Donuts with rainbow sprinkles and bacon double cheeseburgers only from Burger King."

"I still enjoy going to Dunkin' Donuts as well, about twice a week."

"Well, let me get back to work. I got transferred over to the corporate office right up the street from you. I'll be coming here more often. It was nice seeing you, Izzy," she explained, heading toward the door.

"Likewise. Please tell Michael I said hi. Maybe when he's free, I can come pick him up to spend time with him. We have a lot of catching up to do."

"I sure will. He'll be excited to know I ran into his god-mommy today."

"Take care, Rachel."

"May I help you?" I requested from the gentleman next in line just coming in the door.

"Isabel Preston, long time no see."

"Mr. Cowan, yes, it has been a long time." The last time I saw this lawyer was when he helped me with the legal aspect of buying and owning the business.

"It's nice to see you."

"Likewise."

"What can I get for you?"

"Well, a moment of time privately would be nice and a slice of lemon cake."

"Sure, let's get someone to take over the register and I'll meet in the right-hand corner."

"Is everything all right with Opal's affairs?"

"Yes, her estate is well taken care of. It's not the reason why I'm here," he explained, taking a bit out of the slice of cake.

"Why are you here?"

"I'm on another client I have, Mr. Dickerson."

"He must have put you up to this," I replied, changing my attitude from good to nasty.

"I have paperwork for you," he explained, taking it out of his briefcase.

"Eric and I have been over for a while, now. I'm not trying to go back in the past," I explained, shrugging my shoulders.

"Hear me out, please. Give me five minutes of your time."

"Go ahead."

"You're looking at the divorce papers of Eric and Mirna Dickerson. It was final nine months ago," he mentioned while placing his fingers on the date. Eric did get divorced on time in May. The papers looked legit.

"What does it have to do with me?" I inquired.

"Izzy, please give me a minutes to talk. You've been avoiding me for months. This is the only way I knew I could get you to listen to me and stay in one place. Don't run to the back," Eric pleaded, entering into the building.

"I have my listening ears on," I stated, not looking him in the eye.

"Bruce put you thorough a lot."

"You did the same. Do you have a point?"

"First of all, I want to apologize for every bad thing I put you through from the beginning. It was wrong of me to ask you to stick around when I told you I was going back to live with Mirna. I'm nothing without you and these past few months have helped me realize it. You're right, money isn't everything. The divorce is final as you know. I decided not to go back to live in the house and took my chances going to court. The judge decided she wasn't entitled to anything pertaining to the business. The part of the separation agreement stating we couldn't have anyone around the kids didn't hold up in court. I know I don't deserve you even talking to me. Please, find it in your heart to give me another chance," he offered, running his fingers through my hair.

"I didn't say you could touch me. Eric, you hurt me so bad. You made a promise to me not to hurt me," I replied with tears in my eyes, shaking my head.

"I know and I'm so sorry. Please, give me another chance. I love you so much, Isabel Preston," Eric proclaimed, getting on both knees and kissing my shoes in front of the customers and my coworkers.

"What do you want from me, Eric?"

"If you'll have me, I want to be your husband and I want you to be my wife," he explained, pulling out a ring box. Inside was a four-karat oval-cut diamond ring. I stared at him for at least five minutes.

"Yes, I love you too," I announced with a smile. Eric picked me up and swung me around. Everyone in the building was clapping. My coworkers especially were glad, knowing the hide-and-seek game was over.

That same night, Eric and I had sex for three hours, making up for lost time. He missed my pussy and I definitely welcomed back his dick. Also, I dreamed about Opal. We were back in Naples in the same room I had slept in. She gave me a kiss on the forehead, hugged me tight, whispered, "He's the one," and smiled at me. Finally, a bright white light appeared and Opal walked into the light while holding another person's hand. It was her daughter, Carmen. She turned around and said, "thanks."

Two Weeks Later

"Are you getting excited?" Vera asked as we were looking at bridal magazines.

"Yeah, I am," I responded, admiring my ring.

"Have you set a date yet?"

"No, but I would marry him right now without the ceremony, church, wedding cake, bridesmaids, grooms, flower girls, and everything else that comes with it."

"You know, Izzy, maybe a wedding ceremony isn't what you want."

"I want to have a ceremony for the sake of my parents and Grandma Elaine. Lauren isn't even in kindergarten yet so it will be a while before marriage is considered for her."

"Don't do it for them but for Eric and yourself."

"Yeah, I know you're right. Eric doesn't seem to care as long as I'm happy. Now that we're back together, all those months apart seem short. We picked up where we left off."

"Yeah, you sure did. I haven't seen you in two weeks coming to the house, so I know what you've been doing," she giggled.

"I don't want a ceremony. It's not my style. Besides, I don't want to get stressed-out. Instead, I want to go to the justice of peace in Virginia Beach and have a reception for our friends and family," I revealed while nibbling off my leftovers from the restaurant Bravo's.

"You know I'll support you in whatever you decide."

"Thanks," I replied, hugging her.

"Let have a toast," she announced.

"Okay."

"We will toast a happy and fulfilling marriage," Vera proclaimed, raising our glasses filled to the rim with Pinot Grigio wine.

Chapter 55

Eric and I got married on December 13, 2007 at the justice of peace. To witness the joyous occasion on my side of the family was Mom, Dad, Lauren, Grandma Elaine, Vera, and Bernard. On Eric's side was his mother, Vickie, and the two brothers, Evan and Harry. Even though Mirna knew two months prior to the date we were getting married, the day before she whisked the kids off to Georgia to visit her family. Eric was devastated because he really wanted them to be here. Cheering him up wasn't easy, but I assured him we could make many memories to come with Eric Junior and Tommy.

For our honeymoon, we arrived in St. Tropez four days ago, staying in the exclusive Chateau De La Messardiere Hotel, courtesy of Jimmy Risoto as a wedding gift. It's a four-story hotel that consists of three wings, pillars, arches, and tower with spire. The most important thing I loved was the peace and quiet. A luscious swimming pool, sauna, and exercise room were available to all the guests. When the sun set, we walked along the Pampelone beach holding hands. The homes in St. Tropez looked more like castles with countless fresh flowers surrounding it. As an added bonus, if there was practically anywhere guests would like to go, a shuttle bus at the hotel's expense would be provided. Not to mention, the location of the hotel was in short distance of downtown to shop. We have only three more days left before we return to Virginia. I plan to come back again for our one-year anniversary.

Once arriving back on Virginia soil, Eric and I decided for him to move in my house because it had more space for Eric Junior, Tommy and us. After his place is cleaned out, we plan to rent it out to make a profit. Eric is eager to get back into real estate. I reminded him to start a corporation and I have done the same thing with my businesses.

Chapter 56

Life couldn't get any better for myself, so I thought. I had a lot to be thankful for. A new husband who adores me, two handsome stepsons, my relationship restored and built stronger with my parents, and a thriving business. If profits keep increasing, I may dip my hand in to owning a Cold Stone Creamery. The Starbucks and the Tropical Smoothie Café are self-sufficient. The same employees have been with me through thick and thin. Today was bittersweet, because Pam graduated from Virginia Wesleyan and will be working in her field as a teacher. She will be truly missed. I told her if things don't work out with her new job, the door is always and forever open at Starbucks for her to come back.

"What did you cook for dinner tonight?" I asked after dialing Eric's cell phone number, getting straight to the point.

"And hello to you, Izzy. You must be hungry."

"I'm starving," I confessed. Working a double shift wore me out. With Pam gone and Brittany sick, I had to stay.

"Well for you, turkey sandwiches with mayonnaise covered all over it."

"Eric, I won't eat it. I hate mayonnaise. Stop playing with me. What did you cook?" I inquired. I had to admit he was a better cook than I was.

"I have prepared for you teriyaki chicken, macaroni and cheese, Caesar salad with croutons and creamy Parmesan dressing. Oh, I forgot, the cornbread will be coming out of the oven in five minutes."

"Wow, I can't wait to get home. It sounds delicious."

"You've been eating a lot lately. Are you on your period?"

"No, since I've been working more hours, I burn more calories. Walking back and forth to make the coffee selections works out my body. Well, I think cardio at least." Eric doesn't know what to say out of his mouth at times.

"Izzy, you're right. You do move around a lot at work. When are you coming home? After you eat, I'll get your bath ready with steaming hot water."

"I'll be home in about fifteen minutes. We're just finishing up closing procedures. I'm going to stop and get gas on the way. Do you need anything?"

"No, just you in this house with me, tonight and the rest of eternity."

"Since you put it that way, I'll be home as soon as I can. I love you."

"I love you too," Eric stated and hung up the phone.

"Good night, Marcella and Cole. I'll see both of you in the afternoon," I announced while we walked to the car.

"'Bye," they replied in unison.

Almost falling asleep, I still stopped to get gas because I hate doing it first thing in the morning. Tomorrow morning, I have a meeting with a franchise representative from Cold Stone Creamery. Eric and I have discussed this potential move. He's in agreement with it as long as he can have all the free ice cream he wants and we have to christen the store, if you know what I mean. I can't wait, it will definitely be fun.

After I pumped the gas, I went inside the store to pay and get a bottle of water because my throat was dry. The cashier was having trouble with the receipt tape and wasn't able to process credit card payments. Luckily, I had the cash to pay for my items.

"Turn around," a voice commanded as I walking back to the car.

"Mirna, what are you doing?" I demanded to know with my hands covering my stomach.

"You know why I'm here," she answered, pointing a 9 mm gun at me, coming closer. My heart was pounding in my chest.

"No, I don't. Please put the gun down," I pleaded. Mirna looked as if she had not slept in days. She had rings around her eyes and her breath reeked of alcohol. By this time, the clerk and other people saw what has happening. The clerk got on the phone. I was hoping she was calling the police. I knew Mirna despised me but I didn't realize it was to the point where she wanted to kill me.

"I have to get a job and pay bills. The money from the house proceeds is dwindling fast and I don't have a plan B. Plus, you turned my whole family against me."

"Mirna, you need help. Please, put the gun down."

"Shut up, I'm tired of hearing your damn mouth. You stole my family away from me," she screamed and fired two shots. I fell to the ground. They ended up in my left arm. I felt the sting. A woman and her child were screaming. People were scattering all throughout the gas station. I was bleeding profusely.

"Somebody, please help me," I whimpered.

* * *

"Mam, can you hear me?" a voice called out. I nodded.

"Please don't try to talk. You've been shot and we're rushing you to Sentara Leigh Hospital. Guys, she's losing a lot of blood. Get there as fast as you can," the paramedic demanded. With the loss of so much blood, I felt weak and fainted.

Once again, I returned to the same room I was staying at Opal's house, only this time I heard a baby crying.

"The baby is beautiful, it's a boy. He looks like Eric, your husband. You're so young to have been through so much. The book of your life story would be on the *New York Times* bestsellers list," she explained, gently caressing my face. She was trying to get a smile on my face.

"Can I see him?"

"Sure," she agreed, letting me hold him for a few moments. He did look just like Eric but had my green eyes.

"Am I dead?" I asked in tears, almost afraid to know the truth, handing the baby back over to her. I didn't want to drop him because I felt so weak.

"No, Isabel, but you have to go back. Don't follow Jonathan and me into the light. There will be no more violent acts committed against you. Enjoy your life. Many good things are headed your way."

"Is it the name we would have chosen for him?"

"Yes. Do me a favor and tell Jimmy I love him. He's been taking real good care of you," she said, nodding.

"Remember I will always love you, too" she confessed after kissing me on the cheek. I got up enough strength to give Jonathan a hug and kiss. Afterward, carrying my son in her arms, she walked toward the light.

Chapter 57

"Isabel?" a voice whispered.

"Vera," I stated. In an instant, everything came back to me. Where are the kids? Are they all right? Where's Eric? The baby was in heaven with Opal. My arm was killing me.

"Call the nurse, I'm in pain," I cried out in agony.

"Okay, I'll be right back. Your nurse is right outside the door."

"Hi, Mrs. Dickerson, I'm glad to see you have waken up. I'm going to give you some medicine that will ease the pain. For now, I want you to get as much rest as possible. The doctor will be in shortly to examine you," she explained, putting the medicine into my IV.

"Izzy, I know if you could talk a mile you would. Many questions are going through your mind.

"You had emergency surgery to get the bullets out. Izzy, you lost a lot of blood. Your parents, Grandma Elaine, and Lauren are in the waiting room along with Eric and Vickie. Worst of all, you lost the baby. I'm so sorry. You know I'll help you get through this. We thought it was best I tell you than the nurse," she explained, gently holding my hand.

"How far along was I?"

"You were about three months, according to what the doctor said."

"The night at the gas station, I was going to tell him face-to-face," I cried out.

"Eric fell to pieces once he heard the news. The nurse said you can have only three visitors at a time. I'll go get Eric for you."

"Izzy, how are you feeling?" Eric asked with his head hanging down. He had been crying and didn't want to show it.

"I'm feeling weak and tired. The baby is gone. I was going to tell you as soon I got home," I cried out.

"Izzy, it's all right. The important thing is that you are still alive. We can get pregnant again. Our baby is in heaven, now."

Even if I didn't press charges on Mirna Birnes, the state would have picked it up. Once again, my name was plastered on the news. The mayor, Mr. Smith, wasn't happy about how this turned out, but I told him to leave Chief Birnes alone. Besides, it wasn't his fault. Everyone including myself never thought in their wildest dreams Mirna would have shot me. Eric feels guilty but I assured him it wasn't his fault or responsibility, either. She was charged with attempted murder. After a long, drawn-out four-month trial, a jury of her peers sentenced her to twenty-five years in prison without the chance of parole for the attempted murder of Jonathan and me. Eric was granted full custody of the boys.

Chapter 58

Five years had passed. Today was Mother's Day. Eric was with his own mother enjoyed the day with her. He had planned to take her to Sugar, an upscale soul food restaurant. After visiting with their grandmother, I decided it was time Eric Junior and Tommy got to see their own mother. Eric didn't even look at Mirna. Still, today we do not discuss what happened that night at the gas station. As time has passed on, I have developed a healthy relationship with them and would not dare try to take their mother's place. Four years ago, I started taking the boys to a counselor to help cope with the situation. Eric refused to participate. Yes, Mirna tried to kill me; but she's still their mother. Plus, I'm learning how to forgive and not hold so many grudges.

As we got through the security measures of the Powahack Correctional Center for Women, we sat patiently waiting for Mirna to come out. She looked as if she lost ten pounds. Eric Junior and Tommy ran up to their mom to greet her. The boys were grinning from ear to ear.

Since her family wrote her off, Mirna hadn't seen the boys since she was charged with the case.

"I'm sorry for shooting you," Mirna proclaimed as she and the boys sat down at the table.

"I accept your apology," I replied, knowing it would be part of the healing process.

"Thank you for bringing my boys to see me," she answered with tears in her eyes.

Epilogue

Eric and I had a new baby girl named Yasmin, weighing six pounds and seven ounces. She's a truly a Daddy's girl but inherited my green eyes. Eric Junior and Tommy welcomed her into the family and are quite protective over her. The boys are both in the gifted program at school and heavily involved in sports. I have dropped down to part-time working at the Starbucks and Tropical Smoothie Café to focus more on my family.

Grandma Elaine is still alive and kicking. Her disappearing husband, Edward, died and she inherited a two-million-dollar estate. Needless to say, his marriage to his second wife was null and void because he never divorced my grandmother. We make it a tradition to have Sunday dinner at her house twice a month.

Mom and Daddy are still going strong. The bond between them is unbreakable. He has been drug-free for ten years now. Lauren started kindergarten and loving every minute of it. I truly believe she's what keeps my parents so young at heart.

Vera and Bernard had a baby boy named Bernard Junior, weighing eight pounds and eleven ounces. Vera and I make playdates with the kids. She and I are closer than ever and became the godmother of Yasmin. I am the godmother for Bernard Junior.

Alicia died three months ago of a drug overdose. Her body was found in a ditch behind Church Street. Six months later, Alicia's mother died of a heart attack due to her being so consumed with worry of her daughter. I think she died of a broken heart.

Rachel and my godson, Michael, couldn't be better. He's now playing on the soccer team and making honor roll in school. She, Vera, and I do spend more time together.

Printed in the United States
by Baker & Taylor Publisher Services